An Anthology of Short Stories
by

SHAWN P. B.
ROBINSON

BrainSwell Publishing
Ingersoll, Ontario

ISBN 978-1-989296-59-2

BrainSwell Publishing
Ingersoll, ON

Dedication and Thanks

I would like to dedicate this anthology to my son, Ezra. While there are three stories contained in this book, the main one (and the one that takes the most space) is a story that I had a chance to read to Ezra. He was the first in my family to read (or hear) ADA, and still talks about it.
So, Ezra, this one's for you!

Preface

This short anthology contains three stories. The first one, *ADA*, is my favourite (notice my Canadian spelling there), and someday I may turn it into a full novel. It's actually my first serious sci-fi story, and I think it's a lot of fun.

I had originally intended for *ADA* to be the only story in this book, but found out that with printing costs, it's the same whether I print 80 pages or 110, so... why not include more? Which brought in the final two stories.

The other two stories, *Eyes in the Garden* and *Tap*, are actually written as scary/suspenseful stories. I like suspense, but I actually don't like scary or horror, so this is a bit of a stretch for me, but the stories came to me, and I got excited about them!

I hope you enjoy this short little anthology!

Shawn P. B. Robinson

Check out these books by

Shawn P. B. Robinson

Adult Fiction (Fantasy/Sci-Fi)

<u>Ridge Series</u>
Ridge Day One
Ridge Day Two
Ridge Day Three

ADA Anthology

Books for Younger Readers

<u>Annalynn the Canadian Spy Series</u>
Books One through Six

<u>Jerry the Squirrel Series</u>
Volumes I, II, & III
Hat Squirrel's Revenge

<u>The Arestana Quest Series</u>
The Key Quest
The Defense Quest
The Harry Quest

<u>Activity Books</u>
Jerry the Squirrel Activity Book
Annalynn the Canadian Spy Activity Book

www.shawnpbrobinson.com/books

Table of Contents

Genre: Sci-fi short story, suspense, action.

CHAPTER ONE

I opened my eyes.

It took me a moment to make sense of what I saw. Squares. White… or off-white. I couldn't tell.

"Hello?"

A high voice. A woman's voice. I didn't know who she was talking to or where she was.

Movement to my right.

I turned my head, slowly at first. It was as if I didn't fully remember how to move my neck. As I turned, I caught on—the squares were ceiling tiles.

Her voice came again. "Hello?"

I focused on the woman. She wore white. Held a tube in her hand. One end ran to a bag, and the other ran down to my bed.

A nurse. I was in a hospital.

"Do you remember your name?"

Assess: She might not have clearance.
Decide: I have to maintain my cover.
Act: …

"I don't remember."

She nodded. "That's understandable, after all you've been through."

"What have I been through?"

She smiled at me. Her movements were off, her eyes a strange color. "I'll let the doctor bring you up to speed." A door opened, and she looked up. "Ah, perfect timing, Doctor."

I turned to see two men walk into the room. The one I didn't recognize. He was tall and thin, likely around thirty-five. The other man I knew well. I called him "Handler".

When Handler's eyes focused on me, he smiled. "Teran! It's good to see you awake. You've been out for days."

I flicked my eyes to the doctor and back to Handler.

Handler put his hands up and nodded. "It's okay, Teran. They both have full clearance for everything you have to say."

"What happened?" My mind was still a little sluggish. I only remembered bits and pieces of the mission. What I could remember was coming back slowly.

"That's a long story," Handler said as he put a hand on my left arm.

The pressure felt off. I could see his hand touching me, but something wasn't right.

Pain shot through my right arm, and I reacted without thought. I tried to pull away, but I couldn't move anything other than my neck.

"I'm sorry, sir," the doctor said, "we had to put you in restraints."

I tried to relax. The pain slowly eased off, but it had been enough to make me want to scream. "Why does my arm hurt so much?"

Handler gave the doctor a nod.

"Mr. Teran…" the Doctor began.

He didn't know my full name. Handler might believe the man had clearance, but the doctor didn't know everything. I'd need to keep some of my details close.

"You were in quite the accident," the Doctor continued. "When you came in, your right arm was severely damaged, along with your right shoulder and right kidney. A transport accident." He paused, and I suspected he was trying to give me a look of compassion. It didn't come naturally to him. "We had to replace the damaged tissue. Your arm, your shoulder, much of the muscle across your chest, all synthetic."

The thought that I'd lost my arm horrified me. I had heard about synthetic limbs, but I wasn't really familiar with them. People called them robot arms.

Trying to lighten the mood, I asked, "Does that mean I can punch through walls?"

"Perhaps," the doctor said with a frown.

No humor. I made a mental note not to joke around the man.

"You might also find that everything looks and feels a little off. Have you noticed that yet, Mr. Teran?"

I nodded. The movement felt strange, as if my brain shifted in a way it shouldn't.

"How did that movement feel, Mr. Teran? When you nodded your head, did it feel a little odd?"

"It did."

"Good," the Doctor said. He turned to the nurse. "Release him from his restraints. He needs to move." To me, he added, "You suffered a concussion—a bad one. Everything's going to look and feel a little off for a time.

3

We've fixed the concussion, just as we fixed your arm and shoulder, but it will take a few minutes to reorient yourself. The more you move, the more you will adjust to the new arm and the medication for your head. I expect if you do all your therapy, you should be back in the field within a day or two."

The doctor nodded to me and, without a word to Handler, left.

"Well, Mr. Teran, I bet it'll be nice to be out of these nasty restraints," the nurse said with a smile.

I took a deep breath the moment the steel chest strap released. My lungs felt strong and clear—almost healthier than they had in years.

A moment later, Handler was at my side, helping me into a seated position. "You have no idea how good it is to see you getting up, Teran. I've been so worried about you."

Handler and I had been friends for years. As far back as I could remember. He was always there. Even on many of my missions.

I slid off the bed, placing both feet on the ground. If Handler hadn't had his arm around me, and the nurse hadn't come in to help, I would have gone right down. The room spun, and I closed my eyes.

"No, Mr. Teran, open your eyes," the nurse said quickly. "You have to get used to everything, and you can't do that with your eyes closed."

I slowly reopened my eyes. My stomach twisted, my jaw did something funny. The floor seemed too far away.

I was a wreck.

I planted my feet firmly and balanced myself. My vision steadied. My hands stopped trembling.

"You're getting the hang of it, Mr. Teran. It doesn't take long. Everyone's always a little off after going through something like this."

"Going through something like what, exactly?"

"Trauma, Mr. Teran. With the loss of a limb and major organ, you're lucky we got to you so quickly."

The pain in my arm began to ease some more. I moved my shoulder. It felt awkward, but I felt strong. I couldn't help but think I really could punch through a wall.

"Let's go for a walk, Mr. Teran," the nurse said.

I took a step and found myself feeling much better. I put up my hand. "We'll be okay. You go back to what you need. If we need anything, I'll call you."

The nurse's piercing gaze bore into me as if she were trying to figure something out. A moment later, she nodded. "All right, Mr. Teran. If you need anything, just holler. You're the only patient on this floor. You won't disturb anyone else."

I moved toward the door with Handler. He'd always been my greatest support. Today was no different.

Once we were out of earshot, I asked once again, "How'd you come by that name?"

"My parents were odd," Handler explained. "They wanted to confuse me and everyone else."

I'd never heard that one before. Always a different answer.

"My mission?"

Handler nodded as we walked slowly down the hall. With every step, my balance improved. The colors were still wrong along with my depth perception, but I hoped it would all come back.

"You completed your mission," Handler said with a smile. "I don't know what all you remember from the last few hours before your accident, but we believe your infiltration was complete. All that's left is the debrief, and then we can take down Sigma."

I returned the smile. I couldn't quite remember how long I'd been undercover, but I had gained the trust of Marda—Sigma's leader—and had collected information on just about every terrorist cell around the world. We could finally end their influence, their violence, their lies.

We passed a porthole, and the sunlight shining through the ocean waters caught my eye. "I didn't realize we were this close to the surface. We're not in Havana anymore?"

Handler shook his head. "No, we're back in New Paris. The hospital is only about seventy feet below the surface."

New Paris. I'd only been there a few times. Sigma didn't have a cell in this city.

"Where's their main base of operations?" Handler asked.

"You don't want to wait for the debrief?"

He laughed. "No, I'm just curious. I thought perhaps Havana might be it, but many of the higher-ups thought it was likely one of the Asian cities."

"Both wrong. A lot of the action takes place in Havana, but Toronto is the place. Right down in the lower sections."

"I see. I look forward to—"

I hit the floor hard, chunks of the ceiling crashing down on me. I rolled and slammed up against the wall.

Assess: Not an accident—a bomb. Need to locate Handler.
Decide: Get up and get out.
Act: …

I pulled myself out from under the debris. An arm stuck out from under a few tiles, and I grabbed Handler and pulled him to his feet. He was dazed, but I didn't wait for him to focus. The chance of flooding was too great to remain near the site of the explosion.

I dragged him down the hallway, using my right arm to pull him along. It certainly did feel strong, and my balance had fully come back.

We were in a United World Network hospital—UnWoN—so it didn't surprise me to see the nurse step out from behind her counter with a pulse cannon.

Her job was to protect Handler and me.

And my job was to protect the information in my head.

Before we passed her position, she went down in a shower of bullets.

The enemy was inside.

> *Assess: The enemy is armed. It is reasonable to assume that Sigma has found me. It is imperative that I escape.*
> *Decide: There is an exit ahead. Go for it.*
> *Act: …*

I ran hard. At first, Handler stumbled along, but he slowly regained his footing. We'd be out soon.

I reached the door, but my body jerked to the side as something slammed into me. I rolled for a good ten feet or so and sprung to my feet just as a second pulse blasted into me, slamming me up against the wall. Before I could get up, a bag came down over my head, and I felt restraints tighten around my wrists.

I couldn't see a thing through the bag. Multiple hands lifted me, and I heard the grunts. The quick glance I caught of them before they covered my face revealed six large men. Too many to take, even if I wasn't restrained.

I counted the hands holding me. At least ten, if not the full twelve. I hoped Handler survived. Maybe they left him behind.

CHAPTER TWO

We moved through a series of doors, one of which had the familiar hiss of a port, and my footsteps on the metal floor had a unique ring to it. I'd recognize the sound of a subtrans anywhere.

We lurched away from the port, and the pressure in the subtrans increased. We were dropping toward the ocean floor.

"Do we take the bag off?"

I don't think the man who spoke intended for me to hear, but it was hard not to. He should learn to either send signals or whisper quietly enough that the target can't hear.

No response, just movement. The bag didn't come off, so I assumed the answer was a simple shake of the head.

"We've got company!"

I recognized that voice. Sted—a pilot. One of the best Sigma had. He was also one of their greatest strategists. They wouldn't risk him if they didn't think the mission was important.

Assess: Sigma has captured me. The restraints suggest that they suspect I'm their enemy, but the man's question about the bag suggests there is some doubt about my loyalties.

*Decide: I must resume my mission to infiltrate Sigma until
UnWoN can pull me out.*
Act: …

"Wait," I called out, letting my voice sound weak
and a little scratchy, "is that Sted? Who are you guys?
You're…. Oh no, Sted! Have they captured you too?"

No response came, other than a sharp shift in the
subtrans' movement. Sted needed to avoid whoever was
tracking us. I gathered he wouldn't answer yet, but my
question would continue to ring in their ears.

"Drop to the floor. We can lose them in the caves."

The man spoke with authority. I recognized his
voice, but it was muffled. He likely had a mask on to
disguise his face. That meant his identity was thought to be
unknown to UnWoN.

Rick. Rick led this mission.

"Rick?" I asked, slipping just enough shock into my
voice. "You're… wait… what's going on here, guys? I'm
one of you! Why are you doing this to me?"

The subtrans lurched to the side, and the pressure
regulators struggled. We were dropping fast.

"Teran," Rick said, "until we know for sure what's
been done to you, our orders are to keep you restrained and
keep the bag on your head."

The subtrans turned sharply once again. I figured
Sted must have dodged something. Whatever it was,
UnWoN wouldn't use torpedoes. They wanted me alive.

Captured by the enemy or not, at least neither side
wanted me dead.

I took note of how hard the regulators worked as
they hissed above me. They could maintain pressure well,
assuming we didn't drop too fast.

My ears did something funny. Sted would only risk
a drop like that if he thought our lives depended on it.

I, however, couldn't do anything about that. Rick was my priority.

"Hey, Rick, I get that you have your orders, but you know I'm a solid navigator. If we've gotta get outta here, Sted's the man on the controls, but I'm the man to give him direction."

The subtrans lurched again, and I smacked my ear against the bulkhead. It didn't feel good. My head did something funny. I still wasn't back to my normal self.

"Sorry, Teran," Rick replied. "You know when Marda gives orders…."

I laughed. I had Rick now. "Hey, I get it. What Marda says, goes. No one knows that better than me."

He and a few others chuckled as Sted turned sharply again. Rick would trust me now, even though he wouldn't pull the bag. I still couldn't hear any signs of Handler. If they'd brought him, they wouldn't be as kind to him, but I might be able to convince them to keep him alive.

Someone cleared his throat. Gerry. Of course he'd be here. The young man was loyal to a fault, and Rick relied on him for just about everything.

The sound and rhythm of the subtrans changed. We had entered the caves. They were dangerous places, if you didn't know your way through. Sted never knew, but he always managed to get out again.

A few minutes later, Sted called out, "I think we lost them."

"Take us home," Rick responded.

I sensed someone sit down beside me. "Hey buddy," Rick began, "what did they do to you?"

I shook my head, hoping it might dislodge the bag somewhat, but no luck. "All I remember is I woke up in a hospital bed. Don't remember anything before that. But…" I paused and lowered my voice to give the impression that I might be struggling with what had happened. "They... I... my arm..."

"What's with your arm?" Rick asked, the concern evident in his voice.

"They said I was in an accident." I paused again and took a deep breath. I let it out slowly, dropping my chin to my chest. "I lost my arm, Rick." I added a choke to my voice. "They replaced it."

There was silence for a while. No one in the subtrans moved. I suspected that meant they all knew and cared for me.

"Let me check."

I felt fingers probe my right forearm, upper arm, shoulder, and chest. I heard a shuffle of feet across the floor of the subtrans, and Rick felt my left arm as well.

"Hey!" I let out an uncomfortable laugh. "Only the one arm."

"Just checking," Rick replied. "We'll need to do a full scan soon."

"Of course." I hoped Handler hadn't authorized the implantation of a tracking device. Such a move was often implemented on suspects, but not on trusted agents. It would be difficult to regain Sigma's trust if I happened to be transmitting our location to UnWoN.

I felt another shift, and our speed picked up significantly. We were out of the caves, likely on our way to Havana.

That meant I had less than five hours to perfect my cover story. I had to include the possibility of a tracking device and perhaps even Handler's presence.

———————◆———————

The subtrans slowed down, went through some strange maneuvers, and we connected with something. The door to my right hissed, and a moment later, I heard it slide open.

"We're here, Teran." An arm grasped my elbow. Not roughly. That was a good sign. Rick cleared his throat and added, "Marda's going to want to see you right away."

"Is that a good thing?"

"You're a better judge of that kind of thing than I am, Teran. We just have to be sure."

> *Assess: I need to regain Marda's trust.*
> *Decide: Create the assumption that I am more concerned for their security than they are.*
> *Act: …*

I came to a stop and turned my head in the direction I knew Rick to be standing. When I spoke, I let the humor slide away and dropped my voice to just above a whisper. "Rick, you gotta scan me for any tracking devices. I…" I shook my head. "I don't know how long I was out or what all they did to me."

He squeezed my arm and matched the volume of his voice to mine. "No worries, buddy. We've got this. You wrote the protocols, remember?"

I did. And I'd been thorough. Unfortunately.

We moved through a series of corridors. Havana's base was right near two exits—one on the north and one on the northeast. From the turns and sounds, I thought we might be at the one on the north.

Ten minutes later, Rick told me to sit. I was grateful. As strong as I felt, I also knew things were still a little off. The bag didn't help.

"Scan him," Rick ordered.

It was generally something you couldn't feel, but I thought for sure I could sense the scan move across my body. Likely just nerves.

Rick spoke again. "Pull it off."

I blinked a few times as my eyes adjusted. Rick nodded to me before he and Gerry walked out of the room.

To my right, the door clicked shut behind the two men. Ahead, a two-way mirror showed my reflection. To my left... Handler.

I wanted to cry out his name. His chest still moved, which gave me some relief, but his face was a mess. I suspected some of it was from the explosion at the hospital, but the rest looked like a few of the members of Sigma had roughed him up.

He opened his one eye just a bit and shook his head. He was right. Best not to say anything in case I said the wrong thing.

I turned back to the door on my right just as it opened. A woman in her mid-thirties—about my age—walked in. She barely glanced at me, which was far more than she did for Handler.

When she reached the center of the room, about three steps in front of me, she stopped without turning to face me. Her eyes remained on the floor, and a tear streamed down her cheek.

Marda had always been an emotional one around me. Far too open. Far too trusting. Far too compassionate. She had been easy to manipulate. From her, I had gained all the intel and access I had sought.

> *Assess: Tears suggest she either missed me or felt betrayed. The lack of eye contact suggests the latter—grief over a sense of betrayal. Her emotions will be difficult to manipulate, but not impossible. She had always hoped there might be more between us than there had been.*
> *Decide: Match her worry.*
> *Act: ...*

13

"Marda," I choked. "What's going on? You guys rescued me. I get that you had to scan me to make sure, but the fact that you're not digging a tracker out of my leg suggests I'm clean. What are you…?" I paused and swallowed before taking a deep breath, letting my voice come out shaky. "Marda, tell me what's going on. What's changed?"

She slowly turned toward me, keeping her eyes on the floor at first. She bit her bottom lip, closed her eyes, and more tears flowed. When she opened them, she met my gaze.

I was wrong. It was not grief in those eyes.

That was hatred.

I gasped, giving just enough of a reaction. "Marda." I let my voice come out small and weak. "Why… you've never looked at me like that… Marda?"

The tears flowed more freely, and I caught sight of a glimmer of hope in her eyes. I had her. Just a little more, and I'd be back in her good books. The one part of my mission I had failed to complete was to kill Marda. I wouldn't fail this time. UnWoN would likely retrieve me within the day. I had that long to finish the job.

"What do you want?" she asked, the familiar authority back in her voice.

I let my face fill with disbelief and confusion. "What do I want?" I shook my head. "What do you mean? I want the same things I've always wanted." I dropped my voice to a whisper again and glanced toward the door, then the two-way mirror. My hands were still bound behind me, but I leaned forward in my chair. "Marda, what's wrong? What's changed? I…" My eyes drifted to my right arm. "It's not my arm, is it? I didn't have a choice. Besides, they said my natural arm was too damaged. Would you rather I not have an arm at all?"

"It's not your arm."

"Then what is it?"

She walked to the side of the room where Handler sat, slumped in his chair. Without any sign of concern for him, she grabbed the back of the chair, and Handler rolled to the floor. I kept my reaction to a minimum. A moment later, she sat across from me on Handler's chair.

"How do I know I can trust you?" she barked. There was hope there, but there was a lot of anger. A lot. There was also something else, but I couldn't put my finger on it.

"It's me, Marda!" I shook my head and closed my eyes. I let my face fill with grief. "I didn't ask for whatever happened to me. I don't even remember it. I just woke up in an UnWoN hospital. They told me it was New Paris and that I had a synthetic arm and kidney. What am I supposed to do about all that?" I paused again. With Marda, it had never been what I said, but the pauses at the right time. I could see the hope grow in her eyes as I took a few deep breaths. "Give me a shot of alethon. Strap an old polygraph on me if you want. I don't care!" I hated the feeling of alethon in my system, but I was one of the few people who could lie with it coursing through my veins.

"Neither of those will work on you."

I stared at her for a moment, letting shock fill my face. Truthfully, I *was* shocked. I didn't know how she could know that. "What do you mean, Mar?" I hoped using my little nickname for her might help make the conversation less of an interrogation and remind her of what we once had. "Why won't they work on me?"

She let her eyes drop to the floor again and took a deep breath. Something had changed. I didn't know what, but I'd won another small victory.

She turned her head back to the two-way mirror. A moment later, I heard three sharp taps from the other side. A signal—hopefully good.

"Okay… Teran." She struggled to say my name. She must have been more upset at me than I had thought.

She stood and walked to the door. Without looking back, she stopped and added, "Teran, we're taking a chance. Your access codes are still active. You can… step back into your post. But we're going to need to take you to The Canal."

"Sure," I replied. "I don't know why, but I trust you, Marda. Whatever you need. We're in this together. We always have been."

Her shoulders slumped. Yet another victory. It would not be long before I had regained her trust. I wouldn't kill her until I had a means of escape, but that opportunity would present itself soon enough.

When she opened the door, she ordered, "Untie him," and she was gone.

Rick came in and drew his knife.

"Glad that's over," I said. "Do you know what's got her so spooked?"

Rick didn't reply. He moved around behind me and a moment later, my bonds slid away. I ignored Handler, but out of the corner of my eye, I saw him stand, rubbing his wrists.

"We have to move." Rick pointed toward the door. "After you."

> *Assess: Rick is far colder toward me than he had been before. Something affected his attitude. It was either the conversation with Marda, or the scan.*
> *Decide: The conversation had gone well. The scan…*
> *Act: …*

"Was there something in the scan I should be worried about?"

Rick turned his head slightly to me and smiled. "No worries, buddy. There was no tracking device. It really just showed us the extent of their work on you."

That concerned me. "Did they not do a good job?"

He shook his head and laughed. "No worries there either, buddy. They actually did a great job. Doctor Larries checked it over quickly. Their work was top-notch."

"Then what's the problem? Why does Marda want to take me to The Canal?" The Canal housed Sigma's primary medical facilities. They wanted a closer look at something.

Rick stopped and put his hand on my arm. He gripped tightly. "Teran. Just relax, buddy. Trust us. You'd do the same thing if it were one of us. In fact, your protocols call for a lot of this."

I nodded. "You're right, man. Sorry. I think I'm just a little jittery after all that's happened."

He laughed again. "Is the great Teran having a moment of weakness?" He shook his head and chuckled as he started down the hallway. "I thought I'd never see the day."

I glanced back to see Handler following close behind. No other guards. That was a good sign.

Handler shuffled up next to me. He was not a field agent, but he had a gift for assessing the situation. He mouthed the word, "Timing."

I nodded, and he backed off. He was right. I'd need to wait for the perfect moment. Marda would die when I had the opportunity. I had not had the chance to check out what my new arm could do, but I'd heard the high-end synthetic arms could tear a person limb from limb. It would all depend on how much time I had when the moment came.

17

Halfway to the port, the floor shook just slightly. That was no current. That was an explosion.

"What was that?" I called out, adding a little panic to my voice.

Rick ran to a wallscreen and punched in a code. "Marda! What's going on?"

Marda's voice answered back, "We've been infiltrated. ADAs. Get Teran to the northeast subtrans! Fast!"

CHAPTER THREE

"Let's go, buddy!" Rick called out.

We raced down the hallway with Handler in tow. If ADAs were here, UnWoN didn't expect anyone to survive. Those things were like my new arm. Strong, mechanical, and fast, these creatures received their names from their simple, yet direct, decision-making process. UnWoN only had a few hundred of them on each continent—too expensive to make more—but they were effective in ending any resistance.

Despite still recovering, I kept up with Rick as we wove our way through the corridors. If we were heading to the northeast subtrans, it was likely a ten-minute run. I briefly considered running in the opposite direction to make it to the ADAs—they'd be programmed to protect me—but then any hope of Sigma's continued trust would be gone. I had to play my part until there was no other option.

I heard no sound of fighting at first, but then it came. The familiar sound of Sigma's gunfire, and the unfamiliar sound of ADA projectiles as they zipped through the air. I had learned about them at one time and even studied pictures, but never seen one in action.

I lost my footing and hit the ground hard, Handler landing on top of me. I didn't yet know what had happened, but debris littered the floor. Another explosion. It was a good thing we were still far from the outer hull.

19

I pulled Handler to his feet and gave him a shove forward. Rick was on his knees, dazed. I grabbed him with my right arm and lifted him right onto his feet. He still seemed shocked but nodded as we took off down the hallway after Handler.

I turned back to see a gaping hole in the wall nearly thirty feet back the way we'd come. Through the dust and smoke, four sets of red eyes moved forward. ADAs.

ADAs were not only deadly with their strength, speed, and agility, but they were designed to strike fear in the hearts of their victims with their glowing red eyes, humanoid bodies, bare steel teeth, and clawed hands.

I realized just a moment too late that with the dust and smoke, their sensors might not properly identify me. I ran as the zip of the ADA projectiles flew around me. Handler and then Rick disappeared around the next turn, and I had just about made it when one of their darts caught me.

I cried out but managed to keep running. I reached back as I turned the corner. It had hit me on the right side, lower back.

I ran hard and caught up to Handler and Rick. Somehow, knowing ADAs were on my tail, trying to kill me, gave me the extra speed I needed—despite the dart lodged in my new kidney.

I glanced back, and a jolt of fear shook me. The ADAs were fast—and they didn't seem to worry about gravity. Two of them, using their claws, raced along the ceiling, while the other two moved below them on all fours.

I yanked the dart out of my back. At that point, I needed the maneuverability. I would have to risk internal bleeding and hope we could reach The Canal in time.

Another projectile zipped along and just barely missed my shoulder. They still hadn't identified me yet.

We came upon our last turn, the subtrans port only another dozen feet away, when the first of the ADAs reached us. Once the ADAs identified me, they would fight and make it look real to maintain my cover, but they would not seriously harm me. But Rick would never survive an encounter, and I needed him alive. Until I was definitely finished with Sigma, Rick was my best contact.

I twisted around just as the first one lunged for me. I made sure my face was quite visible. It would only need a fraction of a second to identify me and adjust.

I grabbed it with my right arm and tossed it as hard as I could into the wall behind me, my synthetic arm giving the extra push needed to incapacitate the ADA. The next one slammed into me, knocking me back into the wall.

I pulled my arms free and grabbed its head and twisted, hoping to wrench the thing clean off its neck. Instead, the head just spun all the way around. I grabbed under its chin and ripped upward.

The body of the ADA dropped to the ground. I smiled. I could get used to having a synthetic arm.

The next ADA slammed its fist into my chest, but it didn't hurt. Their programming had kicked in. The Robot would understand by now that I was not only their ally but also that I would need to incapacitate all four of them.

I threw the third ADA into the wall and used the fourth like a bat to smash the third as it recovered. Before either could get back on their feet, I rushed into the subtrans.

The door slid closed, the port hissed, and we lurched forward.

Through the glass porthole, I caught sight of an ADA watching us rush away from Havana.

I turned around, and Rick put the subtrans on auto. I thought that was odd at first, but then saw the urgency in his eyes.

Blood seeped from my belly where another projectile had struck me.

"It looks like it went straight through," Rick said as he calmly tied a bandage around my waist, also covering my wound near my right kidney. "We'll be at The Canal in about twenty minutes. You just have to keep from bleeding out until then."

I laughed. "I'll see what I can do about that."

He returned a smile and then moved back to the pilot's seat and took the subtrans off auto while I examined Handler. He was in decent shape and waved me away. I could see the stress in his eyes. He was holding up well, considering.

I moved to the cockpit and sat next to Rick for a moment or two. I found myself reaching for the console out of habit, but I needed them to learn to trust me. Jumping in now was probably a bad idea. I moved back again with Handler.

Only twenty minutes to The Canal…

If Marda survived the ADA assault and made it to there, then I still needed to finish my mission.

———————◆———————

The subtrans lurched, followed by the familiar hiss. A moment later, the door slid open.

Front and center stood Marda. When her eyes landed on me, her expression filled with relief, but then the distrust from earlier returned.

"Bring him, Rick."

I glanced at Handler. He was already getting to his feet. He stepped up next to me and whispered, "We're running out of time. You'll have to take her out soon."

I nodded. He was right. I thought I had won her over, but I had misjudged the situation. The distrust was deep, wherever it came from. I might not be able to keep her on my side.

The pain in my abdomen had lessened. A quick look down revealed the bleeding had stopped.

On the way, I leaned in toward Rick. "Looks like I'm in Marda's bad books again."

He nodded grimly. "Just don't be smart with her right now, Teran. Things are tense. We need to figure out our next steps."

"Of course." I didn't know what we were talking about in terms of steps, but I'd play along. Until my opportunity arose.

I counted the guards along the way. Two or three I could handle. By the time I reached the medical wing of The Canal, I had counted fifty-four. All armed with pulse cannons in their arms and slides on their hips.

The slides concerned me. Rick had one on his hip as well, picked up from Marda after we arrived.

The pulse cannons were pretty common in Sigma. They could hurt, but were designed to knock you down or drive you back. They were also effective against ADAs, but only to slow their advance.

The slides, however, were unusual. A slide delivered a surge of electricity into the target—enough to incapacitate a human and enough to potentially fry the circuits of an ADA.

Either Sigma thought we were about to be attacked by another swarm of ADAs, or they planned on zapping someone. I'd only been hit by a slide surge once. Never wanted to experience that again.

The bigger issue, however, was that every guard had their eye on me. Not on Rick. Not on Handler. On me.

Even my synthetic arm wouldn't get me through all of them.

"In here." Rick opened a door, and Handler and I walked in.

Handler took a seat off to the side. No one seemed to care where he went. Me, on the other hand... I was their focus. The table in the center of the room was obviously reserved for me.

Marda's voice came through a speaker. "Lay down on the table, Teran."

I did as I was told, and Rick strapped me in. I couldn't help but notice that the restraints were reinforced. I thought I might be able to free my right arm, but the rest of me was secured in place until someone released me.

Once he had finished, Rick left the room, shutting the door and locking it behind him. I was not in a good spot.

"Just relax, Teran," Handler whispered to me. "Don't let it get to you. You just have to convince them to trust you again."

I could just barely make out voices in the other room. Only a glass barrier separated them from me, but the curtain was drawn. Three different voices: Marda, a doctor I vaguely remembered, and another woman. I assumed Rick was back there as well.

"The scan... in just a moment..." The doctor's voice was quiet.

"What will it tell us?" Marda asked. Her voice always carried well.

"I don't think we'll know until it's finished," the other woman added, "but we'll know exactly what UnWoN did to him.

"But they'd know we'd be suspicious," Rick added, joining in. "This doesn't make sense."

"Let's just do... and find out... can..." the doctor said.

I closed my eyes. I could figure this out. Something was causing a great deal of suspicion. Something I hadn't yet considered. The arm... no... that couldn't be it. My arm was likely far more sophisticated than anything Sigma had access to, but it was still just an arm.

The kidney... that was it. A second kidney was beneficial, but unnecessary. Many people survived with only one. UnWoN replaced mine—I assumed it was so I could continue to function for them at optimal health—but there was more to the kidney than UnWoN had told me.

I forced down a smile. I knew my employers were up to something. It wouldn't be bad, whatever they'd done. And I didn't mind. I just wish they'd said something. I could be making better use of whatever advantage it gave me.

I heard the scanner start up. It whirred as it moved over me, leaving my skin and insides tingling.

It didn't take long. I heard a gasp or two from the other room, but Marda remained silent.

"Do... see it?" the doctor asked.

"I don't know what I'm looking at," Marda replied. She was getting emotional again.

The doctor's voice came through again, but this time it was louder, and she spoke with more intensity. "There."

"I still don't know what I'm looking at," Marda's frustrated voice came through.

"That's real... that's a problem."

"That's real?" Marda asked. "What does that mean?"

"I don't... but it might mean... Teran..."

"And—" Marda began, but her words choked out at first. "And the other thing?"

25

The other woman spoke again. "We can deal with that. It's not transmitting, which is good. We don't know what it's for, but I can't imagine it's good."

I turned my head to Handler. His face had gone pale, and he shook his head violently. As he spoke, his voice raised in intensity and volume. "You can't let them take that out, Teran. No matter what, that's the key to all this!" By the time he finished speaking, his voice came out in a shriek.

He was right. Whatever it was, it had to stay.

Assess: I'm strapped to the table, but my right arm could likely break the restraints. If I can free that arm, I might be able to free the rest of me before they come in and use a slide on me.

Decide: Marda would have to die in the next few minutes, or I'd never get another shot at it.

Act: …

I wrenched my arm up against the restraints, and within a second, the straps had ripped free of the table. I pulled at the restraint across my chest, but I couldn't get the leverage at that angle, nor could I reach across to my left arm.

I twisted my body, hoping to reach farther, and the strap across my chest came loose. Rick had been sloppy.

I sat up and even the strap holding my left hand came loose. Maybe Rick was on my side.

"Security!" Marda hollered, "Get in there!"

The door swung open as I tore away the restraints holding my legs. One of the guards shot me with the pulse cannon, and it knocked me back off the table and against the wall.

I recovered quickly and charged, but another shot from a pulse cannon slammed me back again. Before I could move again, Rick stepped into the room, drew his slide, and blasted me with it. The last thing I remembered seeing was Handler's terrified expression as he huddled in the corner, weeping.

CHAPTER FOUR

I came to on a table.

A searing pain shot like lightning across my scalp. I cried out, and a group of masked people around the table grabbed my arms and legs.

I struggled, but they were not the only thing holding me in place. Bands held me down, and these were steel. One even ran across my forehead, securing my head and preventing any movement.

"Hold him!" I recognized the doctor's voice, the one who'd spoken with Marda and Rick on the other side of the glass before they used the slide on me. "I've almost got it."

Assess: They're trying to incapacitate me.
Decide: Singular priority—escape.
Act: ...

I pulled and thrashed and struggled, attempting to twist my body and gain even a little. No matter how hard I tried, I could not move.

The doctor stood above my head. A sick feeling of horror swept over me. She had my scalp peeled back and my skull cut open. She was doing something to my brain.

I caught sight of Handler through the various masked people. His eyes were filled with terror, and the tears just streamed down his face. I knew I could count on

28

him for strategy and direction, but I was the only one who could get the two of us out of here.

"Got it!" the doctor said.

I screamed.

My voice warped and cracked until I ran out of air, but still I tried to scream some more. My fingers and toes shook.

I looked for Handler but couldn't catch sight of him. The masked people crowded around, shoulder to shoulder.

"Teran!"

I looked to my right, unable to move my head. Marda stood there. I couldn't make sense of her expression behind the mask covering her mouth. Her eyes looked angry, disgusted, worried... maybe even a little relieved.

"Breathe, Teran!"

I tried. I no longer remembered how to take a breath.

Something slipped over my mouth and air passed into my lungs. When they pulled it away, my breathing had resumed.

"Whoa!" That was the woman I had heard from behind the glass. "Look at that."

Marda stepped out of sight, back where they'd worked on my brain.

My mind raced. I felt panicked. I couldn't think straight. I needed Handler, but he was still out of sight.

"Look at it heal," the woman said. "I haven't put any stitches in. It just... healed up. Like the wounds in his abdomen and back."

Marda stepped into view again. "Teran, can you understand me?" This time, without the mask, her expression was clear. Relieved. Definitely relieved. But perhaps also concerned.

I tried to nod but couldn't move my head. "I can."

"Do you know where you are?"

"The Canal."

"Do you know what we've just done?"

"No."

She looked back at the doctor for confirmation, then back at me.

Assess: ...

Assess: ...

Assess: ...

I couldn't think. I had to do something. Kill someone. I didn't know who. I think Marda. Handler would tell me.

The restraint across my forehead released, and I lifted my head for a moment. I felt strong—like I did before they attacked me. I felt ready to move. Ready to fight. Ready to kill.

Someone needed to die. Someone... but...

"Where's Handler?"

Marda's expression changed. "Who?"

"Handler. He was right over there."

Marda looked at me with compassion. "I don't know who this handler is."

"When you rescued me from UnWoN, he was with me. He's been following Rick and me around this entire time. He was just over there against the wall."

The people in masks stepped aside, giving me a clear view. No Handler. I needed him. Now more than ever. Handler had always been there.

I turned my head back to Marda. She looked different. No longer the hard, angry rebel leader. No longer the Sigma dictator. No longer the killer of the innocent. No longer the butcher of the weak and needy. She was familiar. I knew her. I knew her well.

I gasped. "We're... married..."

Her confused expression came back again. "Um... yes, Teran. We are."

I stared at her again for a moment. "You're not the leader of Sigma, are you?"

She shook her head.

It all came back in a rush. I remembered founding Sigma—just Rick and me at first. Then Sted. Then Marda joined. We'd hit it off right away. We were married within a year, even before Sigma was truly on UnWoN's radar.

"What happened to me?"

"Can we release him?" Marda asked the doctor.

A pause. "I... I really don't know, Marda. I have no idea if he's himself... or... who he is."

That confused me, but there was a lot of confusion going around.

"Release him," Marda ordered.

The restraints came off, and Marda helped me sit up. She seemed weak, actually. The truth was, I could tell she did nothing to help me. I felt heavy—too heavy for Marda to lift.

I swung my legs to the side and dropped down. Everyone stepped back just a little. I knew why. I was strong. Not just stronger than average. I was...

I glanced back at the table. The restraints from earlier had been reinforced, but I had snapped them with little trouble. The restraints on this table were bars of steel, some nearly an inch thick. And the one that had held my chest was... bent.

Assess: ...
Assess: ...
Assess: ...

I shook my head to clear my thoughts. "What's happened to me?"

Marda stepped up to me and put her hands on my arms. Rick, standing by the door, tried to be discreet, but I noticed his hand move toward his slide. Beside him, Gerry stood, also with his hand on his slide.

"UnWoN took you," Marda said, her voice choked as she spoke. "About a month ago. It took us that long to find you. We thought you were in Moscow, then in Berut, then in... well... it doesn't matter. We found you. But, when Rick and Sted got you out, you were... different."

I stretched my neck a bit, along with my shoulders. I certainly was different. Something was off. I was... better than before.

More memories flooded back. "The scans... what did they show?"

Marda's eyes filled with tears, and her lips trembled. She opened her mouth to speak, but nothing came out. She nodded to someone.

A woman stepped up beside Marda. I remembered her. A doctor—a neurologist maybe... or maybe just a GP... everything was still fuzzy.

"I'm Doctor Swent, if you don't remember. UnWoN did some serious work on you."

"My arm, shoulder, and kidney. Yes, I know."

She shook her head. "No, Teran. They replaced more than that."

I frowned at her. "How much?"

She glanced at Marda, who appeared ready to break into tears.

The doctor turned back to me and closed her eyes for a moment. When she opened them, she gave me a look of genuine compassion. "Teran, the only thing that is still you... still the old Teran... is your brain. Everything else was replaced."

I stumbled back against the table. I began to shake my head violently back and forth and raised my fist at the doctor.

A man beside me lunged forward and grabbed my arm, but I pushed him away.

I stared in shock at the man as he crumbled to the floor, a good ten feet from me.

The doctor rushed to his side, checked his pulse. "He's alive. Get him onto the table." She turned to Marda. "I'm sorry, Marda, but you've got to get Teran out of the operating room. I need to help this man."

Marda pulled me along and out the door. Rick followed close behind. He'd drawn his slide, but I was glad he hadn't used it.

"How did I do that?" I asked quietly. "I just pushed him. He was a big guy. Like... well over two hundred pounds. His feet left the ground... I threw him... how?"

Marda put her hands on my arms again. I remembered. She did that a lot when she needed me to focus. I concentrated on her.

Her voice choked again as she explained. "We don't understand it all, but they seem to have transplanted your brain into an ADA's body. We weren't really even sure it was you for a while. We... discovered a tiny chip implanted in your brain. Doctor Swent removed it."

My mind spun, but one question held on. "You still haven't told me where Handler went."

She shook her head. "I don't know who this handler is."

"He's been with me the entire time. He's been with me for most of my life, actually. I remember him with me even as a child."

"Did he disappear when we removed the chip?" she asked.

"I…" The memories of Handler all through my life were fading. I thought he had always been there, but none of the memories made sense. What I could remember was now distant. In all my life, he never aged. Never changed. Even his clothes… always the same outfit.

It all came clear. My voice came out in just above a whisper. "Handler was the chip." Panic filled my chest… or my mind. I didn't know what was me. "Am I even human anymore?"

Marda's eyes dropped, and the tears streamed down her face. "I don't know, Teran. I don't know anything. I don't know what to think or how to feel. Doctor Swent thought it was still you, but she's just guessing. We really don't know. If it is you in there…" she swallowed hard. I could see her struggle to maintain control. In a whisper, she said, "If it's still you, I still want you."

I felt… grateful. Relieved. And horrified that she would have to love an ADA.

"Wait." A memory from earlier in the day came rushing back, and I closed my eyes to try to see it clearly. "When I was in the subtrans… with Rick… I…" I tried to focus on the memory. It was difficult to hold on to it, but I knew one thing. "UnWoN… they know we were headed here to The Canal." I opened my eyes. "They'll be here soon."

Rick shook his head. "How do they…"

An explosion rocked the base. Most people higher up in the city would not even feel the shudder, but whatever had happened was close.

"Report!" I hollered, stepping back into my role.

Gerry hesitated for a moment before checking his pad. "There seems to have been an explosion at the main port." His face turned white, and his mouth dropped open.

"Give me the information I need, soldier!" In a moment of threat, I needed answers.

"Sorry, sir," Gerry said as he pulled himself together. "The entire east end of the base is flooded. East is not an option."

Another explosion, but this one farther away. The man checked his pad. "That's the north port."

"We go up!" I declared. I didn't know if Sigma expected me to take command again. They might not trust me. Truthfully, I didn't trust myself, but there was no time for indecision. I turned to Marda. "Get everyone into the city. We'll meet at Taco's."

Marda hesitated. "But that's the least secure safe house we have!"

I nodded. "Make it happen. I'll explain on the way."

She paused for just a moment longer before passing out orders. Rick immediately went into action. Marda's strength lay in coordinating the many divisions of Sigma, while Rick was the one to make it all happen.

I pointed at two guards, plus Rick and Marda. "You four with me."

We ran down the corridor and turned right, then right again. In a few minutes, we were at a hatch leading up. We pulled a small ladder out, and I spun open the hatch. One of the men with us whistled as I did so. Those hatches were notoriously difficult to turn. I tried not to think too much about why I had that kind of strength.

Once we were all through the hatch, I reached down, grabbed the ladder from above, and did my best to toss it back to the wall. I didn't want to leave any indication we'd gone this way, but I also didn't want to remove the ladder in case other members of Sigma needed to use this exit.

I sealed the hatch, and we raced down a hallway littered with trash and the occasional sleeping man or woman. The lower levels of each city always contained the greatest signs of UnWoN's effect on the world. Their control of every aspect of people's lives and thoughts and beliefs had initially left anyone who did not agree to fend for themselves. In recent years, UnWoN had decided that removal of all dissenters was their only option.

It was the bloodbath that came as a result of their purge that birthed Sigma, along with dozens of other rebellions. Now, years later, Sigma remained as the only surviving resistance.

We covered our faces just before we stepped out among the crowds and entered a street filled with those deemed unacceptable by UnWoN. People here walked cautiously, careful to avoid moving in any manner that might attract attention. Cameras sat on every corner, identifying anyone without a hood and keeping a record for future punishment of all those who stepped out of line.

"Slow down!" a guard bellowed.

CHAPTER FIVE

We slowed, but dared not raise our heads enough to acknowledge the guard. It would only take a second, and my image would be sent to UnWoN's computers. We'd be surrounded in minutes.

I glanced back at Rick. He'd hidden his slide well under his jacket. I assumed his pulse cannon had already been discarded. We had instituted that policy years before. Pulse cannons were far too bulky for travel in the city.

The farther down the street we moved, the thicker the smell. The recyclers rarely worked well at these levels. At least the pressure regulators functioned properly. Moscow had once had an uprising in the lower sections of the city. UnWoN had turned off the regulators for only a minute, and no one below Level Eighty survived.

"Up here!" I hissed, and we ran up a flight of stairs leading from Level One-Eighty-Two, the lowest official level in The Canal, up to One-Eighty-One, then one more again. When we reached the street, we slowed down enough to avoid notice and moved toward the elevators. Once there, we paid our fare along with another sixty or so people, and a moment later, we were on our way up.

I did my best to look around at the faces on the elevator without revealing mine. I couldn't identify too many, but I caught glimpses of a few people I recognized. Doctor Swent had made it out. She rarely left the lower base in the city. She stood with her head down, doing her best not to stand out, along with a few others. I was pleased to see the man I had injured back on his feet and standing beside her, despite his need for her support.

When we reached Level One-Fifty, we stepped off into a street not much different from the litter-filled, poverty-stricken lower sections, although this area was packed with people. One-Fifty was a transfer level. Elevators moved from here to various levels and a train system took passengers to the other side of the city.

The other difference in this area had to do with speed. Since so many transferred to the elevators or trains on their way to work, people often ran. UnWoN soldiers rarely took notice.

We raced off down the street, taking an indirect route to avoid running alongside too many members of Sigma.

When we reached the trains, we loaded on, careful to find a car with no soldiers. We found seats at the rear of the car and kept our voices low.

"Why Taco's?" Marda asked before I could bring it up.

"I know it's an obvious choice," I explained, "but one of many. It's also near the generators. Sometimes transmissions can't move through that area well. I expect we'll meet an ADA or two. Due to the interference, they won't be able to call for help, and we can move on from there to our next target."

Rick leaned in. "Target? I thought we were on the run, not on mission."

I turned to Rick and glared at him. He backed off, and I noticed his hand moved just slightly toward the slide, which I could just barely make out inside his jacket. "Look at what they've done, Rick! They've managed to infiltrate us by turning me into a monster. They'll go to any length!

Do you know what I was planning on doing just before you shot me with the slide?"

He shook his head.

I turned to Marda. "I had orders to kill. The ADA chip inside my brain didn't just give me visions of Handler; my marching orders were to kill you!"

She took in a sharp breath. "Why me?"

"Think about it." I felt the rage build inside. I didn't know if I was still human, but I did feel anger. "If the leader of Sigma steps in and kills not only his second in command, but also his wife, the woman he loves, everything falls apart. We're the only ones left standing against UnWoN." I took a deep breath and wondered if I even needed to breathe anymore or if it was just an unnecessary process. "If we turn on each other—especially the two of us—then Sigma is finished. And so is any chance of bringing UnWoN's control to an end." I shook my head. I think I would have normally cried right now, but the tears didn't come. Perhaps they never would again. "Marda, I would have killed you without a moment's remorse." I clenched my fists. "They did this to us!"

I turned back to Rick. "We are *not* on the run. We are on mission! We will continue to be on mission until we put an end to UnWoN. They have made hiding impossible. We can't strike from the shadows anymore. It's time we take the fight to them."

The train shuddered, and I felt the change in movement. The lights shifted as we entered the station.

"This is it," Rick said.

We made our way to the doors along with dozens of others. Mechanics and divers and pressure technicians and structural repair techs. Farmers and shopkeepers and service workers. The general population moved without passion, without hope. That would all change soon. UnWoN would be held to account.

Half-way out of the station, I caught sight of Doctor Swent and Gerry. I made eye contact briefly with Gerry, but we both looked away. UnWoN's computers analyzed where people looked and who appeared to know one another. Guilty by association remained a continual threat, looming over every public interaction.

At first, we moved east down the street, then to the north, then to the east again, doing our best to zigzag through the area. Taco's was just ahead.

We reached the doors of the abandoned restaurant and walked right on by. After circling around back, we climbed in through a window. Occasionally, we found homeless men and women living inside, but this time, it lay empty. Only the remains of a few blankets and empty cans of rations. From the looks of things, the former occupants had not left willingly.

We settled in out of sight of the uncovered windows in the front of the old store. Smashed computers and stoves littered the old ceramic tiles. The place had been in use when I was a kid. I remembered punching in my order and watching the stoves fire up to produce a taco in just under ten seconds. The place had been one of the most popular restaurants in the lower levels. It could seat hundreds with standing room for hundreds more.

That was before UnWoN accused the Central American leadership of corruption, removed them, and stepped in to show how much better they were.

No one below Level Fifty thought they were better off. Even the soldiers regretted the change, but they, like the rest of us, had no choice but to follow orders—at least in public.

More members of Sigma trickled in. One of the great things about Taco's was the large windows. From outside, they gave a clear view of much of the inside of the store. Any soldiers passing by would just peek through for a moment on their patrols. For us, there were enough hiding spots that, though the store would appear empty from the front, it was anything but on the inside.

After a while, Marda whispered, "Most of us are here."

I did a quick scan. I estimated over a hundred spread out through the store. Perhaps all that was left of our Canal Base.

I was just about to address the crowd when someone called out a warning. "Something's happening in the street!"

I peered around an overturned table. At first, I could only see people moving quickly along—in a panicked run. But then I caught sight of someone. Through the dirty windows, I couldn't be sure, but it looked like Rick's assistant, Gerry.

"Why's he got his hood down?" Rick whispered. "He'll be recognized!"

A moment later, I knew why.

At least a dozen humanoid steel bodies, glowing red eyes and wicked sharp teeth, stepped into view, moving with inhuman precision.

ADAs.

"Out the back!" I hissed, but the first man through the window cried out, and the next one pulled himself back in.

Marda took in quick reports, then turned to me. "We're surrounded!"

I jumped up and spun around at the sound of the windows at the front of Taco's shattering. "Defensive positions!"

We moved around, distributing the slides we had in our possession, leaving a guard on every exit and every window with at least one. A scream at the back of the restaurant drew my attention. Two ADAs moved like lightning into the crowd, dodging shots from the slides and taking out a half-dozen members of Sigma before my soldiers could land even one clean shot.

From the front of Taco's, Gerry called out, "Surrender, Sigma. It's over."

Before I could answer him, one of the ADAs standing next to Gerry shot him in the head. His lifeless body hit the ground and sent a clear message. There was no surrender. There was no joining with UnWoN.

We were meant to die.

"Hold the line!" I called to Rick.

And then I charged.

Attacking them would not convince them that I was the enemy. Their programming would leave them to assume I was merely protecting my cover. They would only feign their retaliation.

As long as they couldn't confirm my chip was gone…

I reached the first ADA, and it made a feeble attempt to fight back. I pulled its head from its body, and then smashed my fist through the skull of the second, destroying its processing unit.

Before I could reach the third, however, I felt the tingle of a scan moving across my body. It rested on my head for just a moment before the eyes of every ADA in the room turned on me.

It had only taken seconds, but I was now the primary threat.

They zeroed in on me and charged. I grabbed the first ADA by the legs before it could attack and used it like a club. I still had trouble believing the strength in my new body, but I focused on the more important matter— survival.

After smashing four more ADAs, the one in my hands managed to swing its body around and attack. It pulled itself around my shoulders and onto my back, raking my face with its claws.

I screamed and grabbed one of its arms, twisting until the entire ADA came loose and dropped to the floor. I pulled the arm off and drove it fist first through the robot's chest.

Two of the ADAs went down from slide shots. Another ADA moved toward me and had nearly reached me when its body lurched off to the side and smashed against a wall. One of our members must have kept a cannon.

I caught sight of a flash of movement to my left, but before I could react, my body slammed to the ground. At a glance, I counted six ADAs above me. They ripped open my shirt. Four held me down while the other two tore into my chest.

I tried to resist, but their grip was too much. I raised my head while they worked. The pain was excruciating, yet at the same time it felt almost... intellectual, as if I had knowledge of the pain, rather than feeling.

I felt different. I thought different. The blood I saw in my chest sat along the surface of the flesh, but the insides were mechanical, controlled by dozens of tiny computer modules.

I knew what they were after. My power cell. I wrenched my body around to try to twist out from under their weight, but I couldn't budge.

I saw it the same moment they did. It was small— it fit neatly in one of their hands as they pulled it up and slid it out of place.

I made one more attempt to...

CHAPTER SIX

It took me a while to understand.

I could not feel. I could not see. I could not hear. There was nothing. But not the nothing of quiet. There was simply nothing.

With no stimuli, I could only think.

The world that had been no longer felt real to me. All had been a dream. All had been a creation of a silly mind.

I remembered my childhood, my parents, my older sisters, my younger brother. I remembered my friends. I remembered my wife. I remembered marrying her.

It all felt like it could never have existed in this nothingness.

I forced myself to concentrate. To understand.

If my brain had been the only thing still human, it might survive for seconds or even a minute or two without the power cell. It was even possible that the brain's support systems had their own power cell—enough to keep my one human part alive.

That thought encouraged me at first, then made me wonder if I could ever die. Would I live on for centuries, long after those I loved were long gone?

My chest hurt.

That was odd.

My face tingled—although just a little. Somehow, I knew it was healing.

The chest healed as well, but slower. It had further to go.

An irritating screech pulled me from my curiosity. I tried to twist my body to get away from it, but nothing responded. The sound grew louder, then cleared. My hearing had reset.

"…heavier than he looks."

Rick often complained, but never truly minded. He thought complaints were funny.

"You've got the light end. Try carrying his upper body."

Sted. He was young and strong, but I didn't think he'd be able to carry my entire ADA torso, arms, and head.

"Yeah, but you have two guys to my one."

Rick had a point.

"Just keep moving!"

Marda. She always had a plan. Always had a purpose.

The pain in my chest increased. I tried to cry out, but my mouth wasn't back up and running yet. I feared I was more computer now than human. I would need time to reboot.

"Look at his chest."

Another voice. I didn't recognize that one.

"It's like it's… healing."

"He's an ADA," Rick said amidst grunts. "Or at least his body is. I suspect the shell they put around his brain is designed to repair itself."

I took offense at references to me like I was a machine, but set it aside. It was now who I was. It was my future. I *was* a machine.

Any question of purpose was now gone. I had one purpose. End UnWoN. Perhaps now I finally had the tools to accomplish my goal. And it had only cost me my life.

Code flashed before my eyes, followed by images and colors. My optical sensors—my eyes, for lack of a better term—had reset.

I saw Rick, Sted, and a guy named Phillip, I think, above me, carrying my limp body. I didn't see Marda, but I heard her give orders to someone. We were on the run.

Marda stepped into view and announced. "We'll reach Header's Wing in just under an hour."

Header's Wing. Considering the speed they were walking, we'd been traveling for a few hours already. It wouldn't be that long of a trip if we could use the public elevators and trains, but carrying a flesh-covered ADA with a ripped open chest was not something typically done in public. They would have had to use the less visible routes.

"Hey!" someone called out. The tone of voice carried with it a challenge. In these unpatrolled passages, there were often thieves, scoundrels, and even gangs.

A pulse cannon fired, and I heard a group of people scramble to get away. I would have smiled at the thought of Marda refusing to even engage in conversation or negotiation with them if I had control of my lips.

I felt sensation in my fingers and toes. I wiggled them briefly but didn't continue. If I couldn't walk, all my wiggling toes would accomplish would be to distract them.

Any thought of not distracting them disappeared, however, when my vocal processors reset. I felt my mouth open and just about every tone and sound across all human hearing came out of my mouth in a matter of four seconds.

The men dropped me, and Rick drew his slide. Before he could shoot, I called out, "Wait!" I took a few breaths, unsure again if my breaths actually accomplished anything. "It's just me. I'm resetting or… whatever my body does now."

Marda came in close. Tears streamed down her cheeks, and she held my face.

At that moment, I realized I was the luckiest guy in the world. Even with whatever I'd become, my wife still loved me.

Her words came in choking sobs. "I thought we'd lost you. We got your power cell from the ADA, and Rick put it back in. We had no idea if it would work until we saw your chest begin to close up and knit together."

I nodded and smiled, pleased that my lips and neck responded. My body was back under my control.

"I seem to still be alive." I chuckled and pulled myself to my feet, feeling strong and well balanced. A quick glance down at my chest showed unbroken skin. I just needed a new shirt. One that wasn't ripped to shreds and covered in fake blood.

———◆———

We gathered in a small, abandoned apartment, deep in Header's Wing.

I sat on the floor just under the open window. Marda sat next to me, Rick in the center of the room, and a smattering of others, including Sted, sat around here and there. The Sigma Council had been much larger just a few days before.

However, eight was six more than I had started with ten years ago.

Less than an hour before, UnWoN had announced the capture and death of every Sigma member—despite our own opinions to the contrary. The masses took to the streets immediately and now a riot was fully underway.

I hadn't realized how much the general populace had been counting on us to end the tyranny, the limits, the starvation, the control. To end the reign of those who claimed to be doing all for the good of the people.

"Will it be enough?" Sted asked. "I mean... will they keep going... do you think?"

I shook my head. "No."

Everyone's heads turned to me. I didn't know if I had a soul anymore, but I still knew what people were like.

"The military will stand. They won't use deadly force. But they'll use pulse cannons and drive the people back."

Rick frowned. "Should we be down there?"

I shook my head.

Sted growled. "Then it's been for nothing."

I held Sted's gaze. "No, it hasn't."

I smiled. For the first time since I'd awoken in UnWoN's hospital, I concentrated on what it felt like to smile. It didn't have the same effect on me. It didn't make me feel better. It didn't feel good. But it did feel right.

"We have learned two things." I made eye contact with each of the seven others. "The first thing we've learned is that the people are not only afraid, but they're ready to revolt. The second thing we've learned is the military is standing strong."

"How does that help us?" Rick asked with disgust. "The soldiers will swallow anything they're told by UnWoN."

My smile grew. "No, Rick. They are us!"

His face filled with confusion. He glanced at Marda as if to ask, "Is Teran really all right?"

I raised my hands and laughed. "I'm not still under UnWoN's control, if that's what you're wondering, Rick. We have a problem. The people are almost uniformly against UnWoN. They cry out for freedom, then run and hide. Unfortunately, the military serves UnWoN without question. The military, however, is pulled from the general population."

I stood and waved everyone over to the window. Below, in the streets, the people pushed forward, but a large contingent of soldiers guarding the elevators stood in a row with pulse canons, firing into the crowd. The elevators were the only way to reach UnWoN Control—aside from subtrans. The orders from UnWoN to their soldiers would likely be to hold that spot, no matter the cost.

"Look at the soldiers. Look how they stand, confident and determined. Yet, they've all been conscripted from among us—albeit at a young age. Many of them walk among us, but few ever speak with anyone—except to challenge someone who steps out of line. I have long suspected they are under orders not to speak with us 'common folk'. I don't think they have any idea of what the average person goes through to survive."

Rick leaned a little closer to get a better view. "How does that help us?"

I turned and grabbed his shoulder, careful not to squeeze too hard with my new strength. "We are the ones to tell them—tell the soldiers what they should already know! It's time they understand that they are the ones who are keeping our enemies in power."

I waved everyone to their seats. "I remembered something in Havana, but didn't understand the memory fully until a few minutes ago. I'm the one who informed UnWoN that we were heading to The Canal."

Rick frowned. "How did you do that?"

"I was quick. I did it when I sat down beside you at the console of the subtrans."

He shook his head. "I watched you closely. You did nothing of the sort."

I raised my hand. It was hard to see in the apartment, but each of my friends gasped. Out of the ends of my fingers snaked dozens of tiny wires. "I didn't even think about it at the time, but I tapped into the subtrans' com and sent a message. It took less than a second." I lowered my hand. "They did this to me. But now, all I need is access to UnWoN's system, and a message to deliver. I now have the means to tap into their computers. I can ensure that every soldier receives the message instantly."

Everyone stared at me in shock.

I felt sick to my stomach. The reality of my lack of humanity crashed down hard. They could see it too. I was a monster.

"I know what you think when you look at me," I announced to everyone.

"You can read our minds, too?" Sted asked, raising his hands up as if to ward off my powers.

"No." I took a deep breath. "I know what you're thinking, because I'm thinking it myself. I'm not human anymore. I'm not what I once was. I might be an ADA. I might be a monster. But to take down UnWoN, we need a weapon. I'm that weapon. And they made the mistake of giving it to us."

I let that sink in for a moment, then started handing out orders. "Marda, you're responsible for coming up with the message for the soldiers. Rick, you find me a console that I can access. Sted, you take a couple people and scout out the area."

"What are you going to do?" Marda asked.

"I don't know. I need to figure out what I am."

They rose and set out to fulfill their orders, pulling in others to help as needed. I found a small side room and had a seat on the floor. I closed my eyes and concentrated on my new body. The strength I knew about. The speed the strength afforded would be handy. The ability to access a computer was a useful tool, but something else bothered me.

Now that the chip was gone, I could see my orders a little more clearly. I had thought I was merely to kill Marda, but they didn't want a simple murder.

If I had murdered Marda, it would have left everyone disillusioned and hoping for someone else to come to their aid. But if I had killed Marda in the way UnWoN had wanted, it would have left the people terrified.

I had been ordered to drag her out into public view, place my hands around her throat…

The thought sickened me, but I pushed through. My hands were to…

I opened my eyes and looked down. My fingers and hands looked exactly the way I remembered them. There was even the mole that had been on the back of my left hand since I was a teenager.

But something else…

The room lit up, sparks flying everywhere, as electricity coursed through my hands and arced from finger to finger.

I was to electrocute her. It had been intended to be such a display that no one would see me as anything but a monster. It would utterly destroy their faith in me and in Sigma and in any future rebellion.

The people's hero was a monster.

I smiled.

It was time for UnWoN to meet their creation.

CHAPTER SEVEN

"All right," Marda explained. "The message is contained in this chip. Not only does the information include all the statistics for deaths, starvation, abuse, and more, but it will show video of the ADAs' attack in our Havana base. I've also recorded a bit of personal experience of our suffering and the general populace. I doubt it'll take long before it's seen by the majority of soldiers across the world." She tossed me the chip.

Everyone watched what I would do with it. I suspected they thought I would eat it or something. I put it in my pocket, and I could almost feel their disappointment.

I thanked Marda, and Rick stepped forward. "I tracked one down—a console—but you're not going to like it. The closest UnWoN console, at least one that'll do what you want, is on the fourth floor."

My mouth dropped open. That close to the surface, UnWoN had more security, more soldiers, and more ADAs than I could face.

"Thanks, Rick. Sted?"

"The riots have quieted down a bit but are still far from calm. They're at a bit of a standoff. We won't get through the elevator. I think subtrans is the way to go."

Marda frowned and put her hand up. Everyone in the room grew silent. "I want to speak with Teran alone."

We didn't have many members of Sigma left, but those we did moved into the dilapidated kitchen. Marda stepped over to the window and stared down into the streets.

"You're up to something, Teran." She spoke softly, but I could hear the fear in her voice. When she spoke again, she was on the verge of tears. "They may have done terrible things to you, but I still know you. What are you up to?"

"You know what I'm up to, Marda." I closed my eyes for a moment before opening them and turning her to face me. "You know it's the only way."

"There's strength in numbers."

I shook my head. "Not this time. The numbers will only lead to more bloodshed."

The tears streamed down her face. "I can't lose you again."

"Then I'd better not fail."

She came in and embraced me. I wrapped my arms around her, although I felt distant. I wasn't the man she married. I never would be again.

When the others came back in, she announced, "Teran is going to the fourth floor alone."

The others grumbled, and Rick growled. "No way, Teran. We're going together!"

"We're not, Rick. I'm the only one who has a chance. If this is going to work, I have to go alone. The rest of you will slow me down, or worse, you'll die."

No one was happy, but they knew I was right. And it was time to move.

"Here's the plan. Your job is to mobilize the people. Get everyone you can to every elevator throughout the city. They should not attack the soldiers, just keep the pressure on. I'll take a subtrans to the fourth floor and finish the job. Remember, the people need to keep the pressure on to distract UnWoN, but the soldiers need to be free enough to receive the intel I'll be sending them—so don't let another riot break out. Keep the balance!"

The men and women in the room nodded.

———————◆———————

I stepped forward in line. Dozens of people gathered in the transfer port, looking to get on a subtrans. There were rarely so many from the upper levels this far down in the city, but today seemed to be an exception.

"ID?" the man behind the counter asked.

I handed him one of our recent creations. I didn't think it would hold up to scrutiny on its own, but it didn't need to. As I pulled my hand back, the tiny wires snaked out, connected with his console for just a moment. It didn't take long.

"Ah, Mr. French, I apologize for the wait."

"No worries," I explained, keeping my face down just enough that I hoped the cameras wouldn't identify me. "Is my subtrans ready?"

"Yes, sir," the young man answered. "Will you be needing a pilot today?"

"No, I will be traveling on my own."

The man shifted in his seat. "I recognize this is an unusual request, sir, but as you know, many are trying to get themselves out of the lower levels due to the unpleasantness happening in the streets. The subtrans you have reserved for yourself seats a dozen. We only have two left and over thirty people waiting to travel home. Are you willing to take some of the others with you?"

I leaned in close. This was no time for compassion. I had to appear as an elite. "Does anything about what you see on my ID suggest that I care about these thirty people?"

The man's face drained of color. He shook his head and handed my ID back to me. "Right that way, sir. Your subtrans is number forty-two."

I moved past the people, keeping my hood in place. It would be unusual for a man to walk through this area with his face covered, but no one would question me. The people on the upper levels were often eccentric.

I reached number forty-two and sealed the door behind me. I had heard some grumbling that I was taking one of the last two subtrans, but no one dared challenge a man who could command such privilege.

A few minutes later, the subtrans creaked and the pressure regulators kicked in at full power. I was curious what I could handle. Typically, if I moved up too fast, my ears would pop, and I'd get lightheaded. Nothing of the sort happened this time. I overrode the safety measures and climbed faster. Still no problem.

One more piece of evidence that my humanity was almost entirely gone.

An hour later, I reached the fourth floor and nestled into a port. When my door opened, the inner lock was still sealed, but a quick swipe of my card with a quick hack of the computer and the inner lock clicked and slid open for me.

On the other side, stood three ADAs.

The first two ADAs lunged, and I hit the floor of the subtrans, cracking my head on the steel grating.

Pain shot up through my skull, but I knew it was only a programmed response. My vision remained clear. My actual brain was fine—well protected.

I twisted my body, and the first ADA rolled over the second one. Before the second could react, I swung my leg around and kicked it in the face.

I rolled to the side as the third ADA came at me and shot my arm out, grabbing it as it flew by, spinning it around and twisting its head clean off. I threw the skull at one of the remaining ADAs as it jumped to its feet, and then attacked the other, driving my fist through its chest, grabbing what I thought might be the power supply, and ripping it out.

The ADA dropped to the ground.

The only one remaining took its place in the doorway. I knew it was calling for reinforcements. Somehow, UnWoN had figured out I was coming, but assumed three ADAs would be enough.

In a way, I felt proud—proud that three of their best was not enough. But the reality of the situation crashed down on me. They would not come so unprepared next time.

I glanced down. Sure enough, it was a power supply in my hand. I charge forward, twisting the top off my new weapon, exposing the terminals. When I reached the final ADA, I slammed the power supply into the side of its head, forcing ten thousand volts through the creature's hardware.

I raced out of the subtrans. My only hope was that UnWoN didn't know my purpose. Perhaps they thought I was merely trying to plant a bomb. If that were true, I would likely head to Havana HQ, one floor up.

I ran down a hallway, turning left, then left again, then right, doing my best to move away from the elevator and from any access ports leading up. I circled around, trying to make my way to the console Rick had identified. When I reached my destination, two men stood guard.

The door itself was not much to look at. It was merely a relay station, but it would do.

"What's your business here?" the one man called out as I approached.

I made a show of pulling out my ID as I moved closer. Neither man asked anything else. If I turned out to be someone of consequence, they would not question me further.

I passed on my ID, but before the man could swipe it through his pad, I knocked him back against the wall with such force that he crumpled to the ground. I turned to the other man, watching the expression on his face change. Everything moved so slowly and at first, I thought something was wrong until I understood. I was moving at the same speed as an ADA. I doubted the man could focus on me. I might not be much more than a blur to him.

I slammed my open hand into his chest, careful to knock him out but not cause serious injury. He dropped, and I crouched next to him. A quick search resulted in his security card, and a moment later, I had the door open.

Inside, I found a small room with steel walls and a solid door on the far side. On my left was the only thing of interest in the room—the console.

Before I could move, my body lurched forward, and I slammed up against the wall. Spinning around, I drove my fist through the face of another ADA, and ducked out of the way of the next attack. Back out in the hallway, a dozen or more charged forward.

I let my system speed up enough that the ADAs appeared to have slowed down, finding out that UnWoN had not just made me an ADA, but they had made me better. I ran up the side of the wall, flipping over the next ADA in line, grabbing it by the shoulders, and throwing it out the doorway, knocking the next four down. I dropped my hand onto the computer console, and the thin wires snaked out.

Contact.

Command: Secure a channel to every soldier, on or off duty.

The next ADA was upon me, and I severed the connection. I threw him up against the wall as three others jumped, slamming me to the ground. I could feel them try to rip open my chest. They were going for the power supply.

I brought my knees up and swung my right fist around, dislodging two out of the three ADAs. The third one went for my face, but I grabbed its arm.

Every move I made was faster than anything the ADAs could do, but there were just too many.

I threw the ADA across my chest and jumped to my feet, grabbing the next ADA and using its body to slam the door closed. The lock automatically clicked shut, and I focused on the five ADAs currently in the room. Three were already damaged, but the other two charged.

I ducked and rolled, coming up behind the one, twisting its head off. I rushed the other one, crushing its chest with my shoulder.

The other three injured ADAs tried to overpower me, but they were easily dispatched.

I put my hand on the console, connecting once again with the system.

Command: Transmit message to entire military, individual comms.

The door bulged inwards as the ADAs slammed into it. I only had seconds at most.

Command: Access chip.

A small slot opened, and I pushed the chip inside. The console screen displayed,

Message downloaded.

The door took another hit and two of the three hinges popped. One more hit, and they would be inside.

Command: Send to all.

The door flew inward. I jumped out of the way, narrowly avoiding taking the steel door to my face.

When I got to my feet again, the ADAs didn't come for me. They moved toward the console.

I dove for the closest one, knocking it out of the way. I hadn't thought that they might send a counter message. If it came from the same console, UnWoN could claim it was all a practical joke.

I threw the ADA out of the room and plowed into the others. I had to keep them away. If I destroyed the console, the message might be cancelled.

I ducked and slammed my fist into the chest of another ADA.

There had to be another way.

I took a blow to the face but then knocked the ADA back.

To my left was a porthole.

I grabbed the next ADA and threw it up against the ceiling, kicking it like a football as it dropped to the ground.

I could see a bit of light through the ocean waters. This close to the surface, the sunlight reached the upper levels.

If the area flooded, power would automatically cut, but the message would not be canceled.

An ADA grabbed my shoulder, and I shook it off.

I dove for the side wall and drove my fist through the porthole. Water rushed in. Cold seawater filled my mouth and ears, knocking me back as the airlocks sealed and the power went out.

CHAPTER EIGHT

Marda pushed forward with the others. They had managed to get another three or four thousand civilians to move against the soldiers at the elevators.

It was a stand-off. No one moved on either side—for the most part.

Now and then, a man or woman would break out of the crowd and charge the soldiers, but a quick shot from a pulse cannon put an end to it.

"Move another hundred over to that side," Marda ordered. She hoped the movement would keep the tension up. Turning to Rick, she asked, "Any word?"

"We're getting something now…"

She stepped over to him. Rick had hacked into the basic comms for UnWoN. The channel was not secure, but she expected her message would come across that band in addition to most other military controlled comms.

A video of the poverty throughout many of the cities flashed onto the screen, followed by the brutality of the ADAs, hunting down dissidents. The massacres, the cruelty, the executions… a people living in fear was evident in just about every shot. Video after video, image after image, popped up on the screen.

Marda watched the soldiers. Most stood staring at the messages coming through on their armbands. They looked confused and unsure.

She sent out orders to the people to back off, allowing the soldiers all the time they needed.

When the video finished, the soldiers stood in shock. Few would ever have seen any of that before. Most of what they were exposed to was colored by UnWoN's unique perspective.

Marda was about to step forward and call for the soldier in charge, but Rick stopped her. "They're doing damage control."

A video popped up showing a group of people led away by soldiers, the report claiming they were hackers who disseminated the false information.

"If they can twist it so quickly, was there any point?" Rick asked.

Marda laughed. "This is the first time the military has been exposed to anything other than what UnWoN has wanted to tell them. Even when they acted against civilians, they were always told the people were the enemy. This is a big win. They've at least heard another side. We now have the opportunity for real change."

Marda examined the soldiers. Men and women shifted on their feet. No one looked confident. Even the officer in charge appeared angry, although not with the rioters.

The seeds of freedom had been planted. They only needed to wait for it to grow.

"There's more!"

She looked down at Rick's comm. The report continued. Not only were most of the supposed hackers immediately arrested, according to the report, but those who had escaped capture had flooded the fourth floor.

Marda's heart went cold, and she put her hand over her mouth. The news was always full of lies, but there was also a note of truth in each report. It would be difficult to fake a huge section of the city flooded.

"Teran," she whispered. "Could he have survived?"

Rick looked unsure for a moment, but then smiled. He met her eyes and said, "I think UnWoN created their own destroyer. But they also created someone who could survive that same destruction. I don't think a little water will kill him." His smile grew. "You're right about the opportunity for change. We're done here. The soldiers need time to question what they're a part of."

She looked up at her husband's closest friend. "And what do you think we should do?"

Rick put his hand gently on Marda's arm and leaned in before saying, "Let's go get Teran. And we can finish the job."

EYES IN THE GARDEN

Curtains.

I turn my head. Old wood. Beautiful paintings.

I don't know where I am. Don't know why I'm here. I feel a little unsteady on my feet.

Raising my hands to my face, I rub my eyes. My hands are rough. Thick fingers. Dirty. But not the kind of dirt that can wash off. The kind that's ground in from years of hard work.

The old floorboards creak as I turn around. A hallway behind me leads to a turn. I've never been in a house this old or this rich. Well... maybe I have. I'm not sure.

I turn around again and head to the window. I've gotta figure out something.

Pulling back the curtain, I suck in a deep breath, trying to take it all in. Beautiful lawn. Green grass. Well manicured bushes. And... people. Spread out. Dozens of them. All in thin, white, flowing gowns. Barefoot on the grass. Pale faces.

No... not pale.

Dead. Dead faces. I don't know how I know, but there's no life there. Not *real* life, anyway.

As if someone tipped them off, each one simultaneously turns their head toward me. Their eyes... their dead eyes... fix on me.

"Close it!" hisses a voice. "Close it now!"

I turn back toward the hallway. Behind me, a man stands pressed up against the wall. He's small. Thin. Old, but not too old. His eyes filled with terror. He struggles to push himself farther back against the wall as if he doesn't want to be seen. He mumbles something. I can only catch a little. "...eyes in the garden. Only once will they ignore... eyes in the garden. Stay away... eyes in the..."

I let the curtains fall back, and the man smiles then steps away from the wall. Everything about him changes from fear to... "Ah, there you are, my friend."

"You know me?"

"Of course I know you! You're my friend. Although I don't remember your name."

"Phil." It comes out without hesitation. I don't really remember that name, but it feels right.

"Oh, right. Phil. Yes. Phil. Phil, of course. I'm Berlie. I'm the caretaker of the inside of the house. Not the outside... no... no, not out there... eyes in the garden. Only once will they ignore..."

I shake my head. None of this seems right. "How did I get here?"

Berlie smiles as he wrings his hands. "Oh, Phil, you've always been here... eyes in the garden. Just remember the rule. Don't let them see you... eyes in the garden." His eyes drift to the side as if they aren't under his control. His voice comes out as a mumble, but I can still make it out. "Only once will they ignore... eyes in the garden. Stay away... eyes in the garden."

I shake my head again.

"Would you like a tour of the house, my friend?"

I nod. That sounds okay.

He rushes to my side and takes my arm, pulling me along. I don't know if I'm a big man, but I'm towering over this guy. He's really small. When I look down, I can't see my feet past my belly. I don't know how I know this, but I've spent a lot of time doing hard work and a lot of time eating food.

"Where is this place?"

Berlie pulls me out onto a large walkway. A railing sits not far from us, and I glance down to the main floor. Below is what I think might be called a vestibule. It's huge. Up here, rooms lead off a walkway which runs around the outside of the massive area. A large chandelier hangs from the high ceiling, down toward the vestibule. If I were a kid, I think I'd like to swing from it.

"As you already know from looking out the window, eyes in the garden, we are on the second floor." He turns to me and frowns. "Don't look out the window again, Phil. Only once will they ignore… eyes in the garden."

"But… where am I?"

"And along here we have the master bedroom along with all the other bedrooms. You stay in the master, my friend. You don't have any luggage, but you can use the clothing that's in there. Just stay away from the windows… eyes in the garden."

"Who owns this house?"

"And this is the library," Berlie says, pulling me along. "You are welcome to use it anytime. If you know how to light a fire in the fireplace, you are welcome to do so, but I can do that for you as well… eyes in the garden."

He pulls me around the walkway, doors leading off here and there and the occasional hallway, all of which get an explanation of what they are from a sitting room to another bedroom, to a playroom for children.

We come to the end of the walkway where I see a thin stairway heading up to another floor. The stairs are rough, the paint on the walls peeling, and the lights are out.

"Where do those stairs lead?"

This time, he responds, but he's not friendly with it. "No, Phil. That's the attic. Upstairs is not for you. No, Phil. Not for my friend." Under his breath, he mumbles, "Only when they're hungry… eyes in the garden."

He pulls me back down the hallway toward the wide staircase leading down. The chandelier hangs above us as we descend toward the vestibule. Each step is hard on my knees. I know I'm strong, I'm used to hard work, but stairs are not my thing.

"Here in the vestibule," Berlie continues, "we have many paintings from…" He steps away from me and peers down a hallway at something. "Oh hello, my friend!"

I'm about to follow him around to see who he's speaking to when he jumps back and crouches next to the wall. "Close it! Close it now!"

"I… I'm sorry." A woman's voice.

Berlie stands up straight. "Ah, there you are, my friend."

I step around the corner. A woman stands near the end of the hallway, right by a covered window. I think she's younger than me. Brown hair. Taller than Berlie, but much shorter than me.

"I'm Marie."

"Ah, Marie. Yes. That's right. I'm Berlie. I'm the caretaker of the inside of the house. Not the outside… eyes in the garden. Only once will they ignore… eyes in the garden. Don't open the curtains, Marie."

"How… how did I get here?"

"Oh, Marie, you've always been here… eyes in the garden."

She looks at me with a questioning look on her face. I shrug. "I'm Phil."

"Hey Phil." She smiles at me. She has a pretty smile. I can't help but smile back.

She scratches her chin then turns back to the curtains.

"NO!" hisses Berlie, and crouches by the wall. "Don't look outside… eyes in the garden."

I instinctively do the same, pressing myself back against the wall, mumbling, "…eyes in the garden."

When she turns back to us, Berlie smiles and stands up straight. "Would you like a tour?"

Marie nods, looking unsure.

"Well," Berlie says, moving to her side and taking her arm, "this is the vestibule. We will first head into the main sitting room. It's a nice room to read in and relax while you await your meals. Don't look outside… eyes in the garden."

She pulls her arm out of his, and he smiles, continuing on with his tour. We move down a hallway, and Marie lags behind. I glance back, and she's pulled the curtain again. My heart races, but she doesn't look scared.

Phil just keeps going, talking about one room or another.

Suddenly, she pulls the curtain back. Staring outside, she looks upset, then lets go of the curtain and comes to join me. "That was creepy."

"What?"

"The first time I looked out, they just looked at me. It was weird, the way their faces are all dead and all. But this time…"

"Yes?"

"They pointed."

I don't know what to think of that, but it makes me upset. I almost put my arm around Marie like I'm trying to keep her safe, but I don't know her. She didn't like it when Berlie took her arm.

I hear a sound from the front of the house. It sounds like a mail slot.

"Oh no, oh no, oh no." Berlie rushes by. "Oh no... eyes in the garden. Only once will they ignore... eyes in the garden."

We both follow. When we catch up, he's at the front door, reading a note. He opens the mail slot and slides the note out.

Turning back to us, his eyes are sad, but he smiles. "How about some tea, yes? Eyes in the garden."

We follow Berlie to the parlor. We sit. Marie... she's kind of pretty. Like, not a little pretty. Really pretty. But... women like her don't consider men like me. I'm... I don't know what I am. But I'm too rough for her. She smiles at me, though. Again. Sweetly.

Berlie comes out of the kitchen with a tray, mumbling to himself, "Only once will they ignore... eyes in the garden. Now they're hungry... eyes in the garden."

He sets a cup in front of me, one in front of Marie, and takes one for himself. I don't know if I like tea. I taste it. I still don't know if I like it. Marie seems to, though, so I don't complain.

We chat, but I feel sleepy. I think it's the fire. I lean back. More sleepy. Berlie takes the cup from my hand and Marie's from her hand. Her eyes are closed.

Berlie takes Marie's arm. She sits forward, eyes barely open. I don't know what's going on. Can't really move. I think Berlie is saying something, though. His words are clear, but I'm confused. "Only once will they ignore... eyes in the garden. Now they're hungry... eyes in the garden. They want you, eyes in the garden."

I come to, staring at the fireplace. So peaceful.

"Ah, Phil, you're awake, my friend... eyes in the garden."

I turn. Berlie enters the room, wringing his hands, mumbling, "Only once will they ignore... eyes in the garden."

"Where's Marie?"

Berlie frowns and shakes his head. "Who?" Under his breath, he adds, "only once will they ignore... eyes in the garden."

I remember her. But I'm not sure I do. Maybe it's just me and Berlie.

"Hello? Hello? Is anyone here?"

I stand. I'm still groggy from my nap.

"Oh, hello my friend!" Berlie rushes to a woman's side and takes her arm.

"Hello." The woman looks unsure. "I'm Alice."

"Hello Alice, I'm Berlie." He squeezes her arm. "Don't look outside, Alice... eyes in the garden."

She gives an uncomfortable laugh. "Okay, Berlie." She looks at me. "Who are you?"

She's young. Really young. I'd say she's early twenties. Looks like a kid to me. Maybe I'm old. "I'm Phil. I'm... I've been here a while."

"Where are we?"

I shake my head. I'm guessing my face reveals what I'm thinking inside—that I have no idea where I am.

"Well... who are you people?"

Berlie pulls her arm, but she yanks it out. "What are you doing?"

Berlie grabs her arm again, but I put my large hand on his tiny shoulder. He backs off. "Leave the little lady."

She glares at me. "I'm not a 'little lady'!"

"Sorry, miss. I…" I'm pretty sure I don't know how to speak to a young woman.

She turns to Berlie. "Who are you and what gives you the right to bring me here?"

Berlie wrings his hands and mumbles, "Angry people look outside… eyes in the garden."

"You can't keep me here!" she hollers and runs for the door.

I try to go after her. I can't move fast, and my knees flare up with pain, but I push myself as hard as I can.

I get to her too late. She swings open the front door. I see them. They turn to look at us. I see Marie. She's so pretty, but I… I think she's not alive. She's looking at me. Her arm comes up. They all point.

"Who are they?" Alice asks with a tremor in her voice. "Why are they pointing at us?"

I know they aren't pointing at us.

They're pointing at me. I reach past her and slowly close the door. I don't understand, but I know something bad is coming.

Who was Marie? How do I know her? Why was she out there?

The mail slot opens, and a piece of paper comes through. I'm not the most agile man. I try to reach down, but my back is tight. The note slips away. Berlie has it. He reads it, slips it out the mail slot, then smiles at me.

"Phil, Alice, would you like some tea?"

Alice and I follow Berlie to the parlor. I don't know why I'm nervous, but I am. Alice is angry, but shaken from… something. I don't know what.

Berlie hands me a cup. I drink it. I don't know if I like tea, and now that I've taken a sip, I still don't know. It makes me feel funny.

Berlie's at my side. Alice has fallen asleep. No wonder. She must be tired. I'm tired too, but Berlie needs me.

"They are hungry... eyes in the garden."

I groan as I heft my weight out of the chair. I'm not steady on my feet, but I'll make it.

"Only once will they ignore... eyes in the garden."

The stairs are hard on my knees, but I work my way to the top. Berlie needs me. When a friend needs you, you come through for him. That was my rule... I think. We move down the hallway. I have to stop and lean against the wall, but Berlie pulls me along.

"Shouldn't have let them see you... eyes in the garden."

We reach another set of stairs. I remember them. The attic. Don't know what's up there. I thought they weren't for me.

"Losing my friend... eyes in the garden. Don't want him to go... eyes in the garden."

Berlie gives me a little push. I'm not sure I can make it up another set of stairs, but a friend needs me to do it. I'll do what I must.

The walls spin. My head feels too heavy. But Berlie needs me.

His voice is faint, but I hear his mumbling. "Going to miss Phil... eyes in the garden."

I reach the top of the stairs. The door handle is hard to focus on. I miss it once, then twice, then grab it. The handle turns.

———————◆———————

The grass feels cool on my toes. I think I remember pain, maybe my knees, but it's not there anymore. Marie is here. So is everyone else. We're all here.

But I'm hungry. I want more.

Movement in a window. A curtain shifts. I don't recognize the man, yet. Only the first time I've seen him. In the background… behind him… my eyes in the garden see Alice. I want Alice. I'm hungry.

We all point at Alice. It's Alice's turn.

Come, Alice. Come to us… the eyes in the garden.

[1]I pulled a little harder on the door handle than I should have, and my hand slipped off. The unexpected movement brought me back to the moment, clearing my thoughts.

I had been daydreaming about taking a nap. Naps had turned out to be what I looked forward to most in recent months. Hours could slip by without the constant weight of boredom on my shoulders. From day to day, one shift blurred into the next.

I grabbed the handle and turned it. The door easily swung open. My flashlight came out, and I checked the room. As of a month ago, I had stopped turning on the lights when doing my rounds. Having to check out a room with a flashlight seemed far more interesting than scanning a well-lit room.

I moved on with my rounds and stopped in the narrow corridor connecting Sections B and C to look out a tiny window, my only proof that the world outside still existed. The night was clear, and despite my hatred for the cold, the view of our little area of Antarctica was stunning.

---

[1] Tap, written by Shawn P. B. Robinson, was originally published in Nightmares of Strangers: An Anthology of Eerie, Strange, and Spooky Stories by Touchpoint Press © 2021.

The sky always captured my emotions, deep black and broken only by the southern constellations. That night, even the wind was unusually still.

My eyes drifted down toward the snow just below the thick glass which separated me from the sub-zero temperatures. I found myself fixated on an area at ground level.

Even at night, the white snow stood out, but below the window, a small black shape, not much bigger than me, hovered on the snow. I thought it might be a shadow, but I'd never seen anything so dark. At the same time, the blackness moved. I wasn't sure what I was looking at, but something in the darkness swirled around.

I pushed my nose up against the cold glass but stumbled back as the entire mass of blackness lurched up against the wall of the compound. A faint sound broke the silence.

Tap, Tap, Tap.

"What are you doing?"

Upon seeing Jeff, the tension melted away. "Hey, Jeff. Sorry, I... Hey, take a look out the window."

"What happens when I look out the window?" Jeff smiled, but his eyes revealed his suspicion.

"Nothin'. Just look. It's... weird."

Jeff moved toward the window, still eyeing me with suspicion. His large build and height made me look like a child next to him. He bent down and stared out for a moment before he pulled back. He glared at me with boredom mixed with disappointment. "That was fascinating. Let's keep moving."

"No, wait," I pushed my face back up against the window and scanned the ground, but the dark shadow was gone. I turned to Jeff and shook my head. "Sorry, I guess I was seeing stuff."

"You've lasted longer than most. I started seeing stuff the first week."

"Like what?"

Jeff chuckled. "Like dinner. That's what I live for down here. Come on, Eric. Let's finish our rounds, and you can let me beat you at backgammon again."

He moved off down the corridor toward Section C. The thin corridors joining research, command, and living quarters required that we walk single file through the area, but the passage widened out once we entered Section C.

We checked each of the laboratories, and they were all securely locked. Section C was always quiet at that time of the night. We entered the corridor leading through to Section D.

When we reached the end of the narrow corridor, I heard it again.

Tap, Tap, Tap.

I rushed to a window and peered out. I couldn't see the dark shape again, so I jumped to the other side of the corridor and strained to see all around the area. I wasn't sure—it disappeared so fast—but I thought I saw a large dark shape move off toward Section D.

"Did you hear that?" I asked.

"What?" Jeff's bored look quickly changed to an irritated one. "This?" He reached over to the glass with his hand and knocked, *Tap, Tap, Tap.* He shook his head at me. "If you think I'm going to fall for that, they've tried that on me countless times. Nobody's out there."

He turned and moved on to Section D, and I hurried after him. I knew Jeff well enough to know I'd never convince him. He either believed something, or he didn't.

We checked the doors throughout Section D. Section D, the largest of the five sections of the base, contained most of the high-security research.

"Hey, looks like Dr. Reynolds's lab is the only one in use tonight." Jeff said, pointing to one of the labs near the end. "Ever wonder what they do in there?"

I opened my mouth to answer, but from the look on Jeff's face, he didn't care what they did. Sometimes he just talked for no other reason than to say something.

We started back. All that was left was to report to command, and our shift was done.

Just as we reached the corridor leading back to Section C, an ear-splitting alarm broke the silence. I covered my ears and instinctively crouched down. When I got my wits about myself again, Jeff was spinning around, trying to determine the cause of the alarm.

"Down there!" I hollered, pointing toward a red light above the door to Dr. Reynolds's lab and cringing as the sound blared in my ear. I had never been on the base when an alarm had gone off. My ears quickly began to ache from the sound.

When we reached the lab, I yanked on the door handle without thinking, but the lock held. I scanned the empty scrub room through the glass barrier for anything out of the ordinary.

Jeff leaned in and pressed the intercom button. Screams filled the hallway, and my face felt numb. I didn't know if I wanted to break the glass or run back to command. Jeff stood frozen, mouth open, staring at the button. I grabbed his arm and hissed, "Say something, Jeff!"

Jeff shook his head. His eyes focused, and he cleared his throat. "This is security. What's going on in there?"

No one responded, aside from the continued screams. Neither of us had access to the lab. Our orders were to check to confirm all labs remained locked, but never to go in.

"Report!" came a voice over the radio.

Jeff grabbed his radio and brought it up to his mouth as he waved at a camera on the wall. "I'm sorry, Dr. Eds, I don't know what's happening. The alarm went off in Dr. Reynolds's lab, but we can't get in."

"Don't go in there!" Dr. Eds hollered back over the radio. "No matter what, you aren't cleared for that room."

"I understand, sir," Jeff replied. "Is there anything we can do?"

Before any reply could come, Dr. Reynolds barreled into the scrub room, knocking two trays off a counter and scattering sterilized scalpels across the floor. A wild look covered his face, and blood seeped from a gash near his left temple.

He rushed to the door and tried to pull it open, but it didn't budge. He screamed out in fear as he looked over his shoulder for a moment before grabbing his ID badge from his white jacket and sliding it across the security scanner on his side of the door.

I heard a quiet, yet low, beep as it denied him access. Dr. Reynolds began to weep. He slid it along the scanner a second time and typed something on a keypad. The scanner merely beeped again.

His eyes met mine, and he screamed, "GET ME OUT OF HERE!"

Jeff jumped forward and grabbed the door handle. He yanked as hard as he could, but the door didn't budge. He brought his radio up again.

"Dr. Eds, Dr. Reynolds is stuck in his lab. He's injured. His badge isn't unlocking the door. Can you override?"

We waited for a reply, but nothing came at first. Dr. Reynolds continued to weep, looking back over his shoulder toward his lab every few seconds. I could barely hear his next word through the glass, but in a quiet, shaky voice, he pleaded, "Hurry!"

After nearly a minute, Dr. Eds voice came over the radio, cold and resigned. "Jeff, your orders are to move out of Section D immediately and seal off the section. You and Eric will then coordinate the quarantine of Section C."

Jeff shifted on his feet. "I understand, sir—but what about Dr. Reynolds?"

Dr. Reynolds's breathing sped up. I feared he was about to hyperventilate. He swiped his ID and pulled on the door handle once again.

When Dr. Ed's voice came again, it was quiet. "Leave him."

Jeff raised his radio to his mouth again, but then hesitated. I turned my head to see what he was looking at, and my breath caught in my throat.

A thick black fog crept along the floor. It was only about two or three inches thick. It came into the room about a foot or so, moving like a thick smoke, and stopped.

Dr. Reynolds spun around and pushed himself back against the locked door. He remained still. His shoulders barely moved with each breath.

I stared at the blackness with a mixture of terror and wonder. I was sure it was the same thing I saw through the window, out on the snow. While it was completely black and entirely featureless, I could also see something writhing and surging back and forth inside.

The blackness began to swell, growing thicker and deeper by the second. It expanded upwards until it sat closer to two or three feet deep.

By this time, Dr. Reynolds had reached a point of hysteria. His head shook back and forth, and his moans grew louder by the second. He'd given up on remaining still.

I screamed involuntarily as the blackness lunged forward and filled the floor of the room, covering up to Dr. Reynolds's waist. The moment it touched him, he stopped weeping. Instead, his body tensed for a few seconds, then relaxed. He slowly turned around until he faced me.

"I'm okay," he whispered. "It didn't kill me."

When I saw the calmness on his face, my whole body relaxed. My breathing began to slow. I felt like I wanted to collapse on the floor in relief.

Dr. Reynolds's right hand came slowly up toward the window in the door. With a smile on his face, he reached out toward the glass and knocked.

Tap, Tap, Tap.

The room plunged into darkness

"Dr. Reynolds!" I shrieked.

Tap, Tap, Tap.

Dr. Eds voice came over the radio in a scream. "Get out of there! I'm sealing off the section whether you're in it or not!"

Jeff grabbed me by the arm and pulled me toward the corridor. It didn't take long before I ran just as hard as him. Ahead of us, the door leading into the corridor began to slide closed. Jeff reached it in plenty of time and scrambled through. I ran as hard as I could but tripped in my panic, knocking the wind out of me. By the time I struggled to my feet, the door was over half-closed.

I jumped, twisting my body, hoping to make it through. I felt the door snag on one foot, but strong hands wrenched me the rest of the way. I crumpled to the ground on the other side of the sealed door.

"Get up!" Jeff cried.

We raced to the other end. Once in Section C, the door on that side of the corridor closed. A red light came on above the door to indicate a quarantine and full seal was in effect.

Jeff shook as he leaned against the door, peering through the tiny porthole. He stared down the corridor for a moment before he stepped back and looked directly at me. I instinctively stepped back. I had never seen Jeff so unhinged.

"We just left him there." His voice trembled, and he began to ramble. "Maybe he's okay. He looked okay... the last we saw him. He's probably fine. So is everyone else. We're probably all okay."

"Is the door sealed?" Dr. Eds voice called out over the radio.

"I'm sure they're fine," Jeff mumbled to himself. "Maybe they have another way out. Maybe this is all some sort of joke."

I grabbed my radio. "The door is sealed, sir. We made it through, and the door registers that the lock is airtight. Uh..." I hesitated, unsure what else to say. "Orders?"

"Remain there for the moment. I want you to keep an eye down the corridor. If you see anything out of the ordinary, report it immediately. Security is moving everyone to the hanger."

"Yes, sir."

I looked back through the window. Nothing in the corridor seemed "out of the ordinary," but then again, I no longer thought I knew what was "ordinary."

I turned back to Jeff. He continued to mumble to himself as he paced back and forth. I decided to let him be and instead leaned up against the airlock and peered down the sixty-foot corridor joining the two sections.

Then the lights back in Section D blinked out.

I didn't think that was part of the quarantine procedure.

I moved to the left of the door and peered out an exterior window. Outside, the snow shone brightly in the dark night, and I had a clear view of the outer walls of Section D. I saw the lights on the outside were all still lit, but I could only see darkness through all the windows. I reached for my radio to call and ask Dr. Eds if he had shut off the power when a thought hit me. I didn't want to believe the darkness in Dr. Reynolds's lab had escaped— but what if it had?

I rushed back to the window in the airlock.

A thick wall of blackness sat at the far end of the corridor, completely covering the door to Section D.

My knees grew weak, forcing me to lean against the door for support. I kept my eyes on the darkness as I grabbed my radio. "Dr. Eds," I began. "The... blackness... what we saw in Dr. Reynolds's lab... it's in the corridor between Sections C and D. What are your ord—"

I pulled back as the blackness jumped forward. I slammed into Jeff, and the two of us hit the floor.

Scrambling to my feet, I rushed back to the window. The blackness had indeed jumped forward, but not the entire way. It had come around halfway and just stopped, creating a wall of black through which nothing could be seen on the other side. The surface of the blackness rippled like something wanted to break through to us, and with a sick feeling in my stomach, I wondered if it was the scientists.

"What happened?" Dr. Eds cried out over the radio.

I didn't think I could explain what I saw, but I tried. "Sir, the blackness... it... jumped. It jumped about thirty feet down the corridor. Now it's just sitting there."

At that moment, the blackness jumped again, reaching the door before me. At first, it made no sound.

But then I heard it again.

Tap, Tap, Tap.

"They're in there!" Jeff called out. "We have to open the door!"

He rushed to the keypad to enter the security override, and I grabbed his shirt, pulling back as hard as I could. Jeff easily tossed me aside, but just before he reached the keypad, he stopped.

I climbed back to my feet and watched my friend, waiting for him to make a move.

He straightened his back and slowly turned around. I recognized the look. A few minutes before, I'd seen it on Dr. Reynolds's face. My gaze dropped to the floor, and I stopped breathing.

The blackness spread out from the bottom of the doorway. It was only an inch or two deep, but Jeff stood right in the middle of it.

Jeff looked directly at me and smiled. I watched as his arm reached out to the side as if he did not even know it was moving. When his hand reached the wall, he knocked.

Tap, Tap, Tap.

I turned and ran. I had no idea what was going on, but I didn't want that stuff touching me. I glanced back over my shoulder. Where Jeff had been standing was now a solid wall of blackness.

I looked over my shoulder again when I reached the corridor leading back to section B. The wall of blackness had already covered half the distance.

"I'm in the corridor between B and C!" I cried out over the radio. "Seal the door leading out of C and prepare to seal the door leading into B!"

When I raced out of the corridor, the door behind me slid shut. A moment later, the red light came on.

The loudspeaker blared, "Sections B, C, and D are now off-limits. Please evacuate to the hanger. Sections B, C, and D…"

Even above the sound of the loudspeaker, I heard it.

Tap, Tap, Tap.

I spun around and cried out. The window leading back into the corridor revealed a solid blackness on the other side of the door.

"Get out of there, Eric!" Dr. Eds hollered through the radio.

I ran again.

The route through Section B was anything but direct. The hallways zigzagged, and I was so scared I made a wrong turn and almost ran back toward Section C. I turned around and made sure I took the proper route, heading directly to command.

I moved down the corridor as the airlock sealed behind me. Ahead of me, I could hear an argument well underway.

When I stepped into the room, the normally busy Command Center was empty, save two people. In the center of the room, Dr. Ling stood, poking her finger into Dr. Eds's chest.

"I will not abandon my research!" she declared. "We can salvage this!"

"How do you figure we're going to do that, Beth?" Dr. Eds snapped. "It's already out! You couldn't contain it in the lab. You think we can capture it once it's loose on the base? I'm initiating Gamma Directive."

I had never heard of Gamma Directive, but that didn't surprise me. I operated on a need-to-know basis. I didn't even know what the scientists were studying.

"We'll lose everything!" Dr. Ling screamed.

Dr. Eds stepped forward, forcing Dr. Ling to stumble back. When he spoke, his voice came out in a growl. "We've already lost everything. The only thing we have left is our lives. We're leaving!"

TRP

Dr. Eds turned to me. "Eric, Dr. Ling is ordered off the base. If she resists, pick her up and throw her outside without a suit."

My head swung back and forth between Dr. Eds and Dr. Ling. Dr. Eds stared expectingly for me to obey. Dr. Ling looked like she dared me to try.

Before I could figure out how to react, Dr. Ling shook her head. "Fine! But this is on you, Terry. All our research is gone, and you're on the line for it."

She stormed off toward the exit leading to the hanger, mumbling something under her breath.

Tap, Tap, Tap.

I spun around. Whatever it was that was trying to escape had reached the hatch.

Dr. Eds grabbed me and shoved me toward the exit. I stumbled forward, catching sight of Dr. Ling for just a second before she disappeared through the open door. I glanced back just before entering the same corridor but came to a halt.

"Dr. Eds!" I hissed. "We need to move!"

He remained where he stood. His eyes slowly raised to meet me, and he smiled. My eyes lowered.

Around his feet swirled a shallow layer of black.

His hand, seeming to move on its own, reached out to the back of his chair in the center of the room.

Tap, Tap, Tap.

I ducked into the corridor and manually slid the door closed. Once the door clicked shut, I punched in my security code, and the red light came on. Before I could turn away, the window went black.

I sprinted down the corridor and out into the hanger, then sealed the door behind me. When I turned around, I came face to face with Dr. Ling.

"Where's Dr. Eds? Wasn't he right behind you?" As angry as she had been a moment before, she showed only concern now.

I shook my head and grabbed her arm. I pulled her along the hallway and concentrated on getting Dr. Ling out. From what I'd seen, we didn't have much time.

As I ran, I asked her, "What do I need to know about this... whatever it is?"

"Don't let it touch you," she answered, her voice betraying her fear. "The cold slows it down, so we might be able to escape if we get outside. But whatever happens, just don't let it touch you!"

We exited the hallway just as I heard it again.

Tap, Tap, Tap.

The main hanger was large enough to store a couple of airplanes, but it rarely housed anything like that. At that moment, there were only around a dozen people still inside. They scrambled to put on their suits, gloves, and boots. A lit display above one of the doors informed us that the outside temperature that night held at -72 Fahrenheit.

I rushed into the prep room and grabbed one of the many thick full-body suits, along with boots and gloves. I ran back out into the main hanger, dropped everything on the floor, pulled on my suit, sat down, and yanked off my shoes. A moment later, I had one boot on and struggled to tie up the laces. Bodies rushed past. The room cleared. Soon, only Dr. Ling, a young guy I didn't know, and myself were left.

I finished tying my first boot.

Tap, Tap, Tap.

Dr. Ling's head shot up, and we both looked back toward the other sections of the base. A woman stood in the hallway that Dr. Ling and I had just come through. She must have been slower than everyone else to evacuate. At first, I didn't know why she wasn't running, but then I saw her reach for the wall.

I quickly focused on my second boot as I heard the faint, *Tap, Tap, Tap.* The ties were thick and difficult to work with, and I fumbled with them in my panic.

Tap, Tap, Tap.

I looked up. The wall of blackness stood only a hundred and fifty feet away from us.

Tap, Tap, Tap.

The blackness jumped toward us, stopping around a hundred feet away. The young guy and Dr. Ling both scrambled to their feet and out the door.

Tap, Tap, Tap.

I got to my feet and ran, zipping up my suit and pulling on my gloves, and rushed out the door into the bitter cold. I slammed the door shut behind us and stumbled back into the snow.

The young guy stood outside the door. I scrambled to my feet and gave him a shove. "We have to move!"

The last few people to leave the main base were already on their way toward our designated evacuation point, the Shed, along with Dr. Ling and the young guy. I started after them, but before taking more than a few steps, a loud, deafening, *"Tap, Tap, Tap,"* resounded through the air. Whatever the blackness was after, it had reached the large hanger door. The entire door shook, and the sound echoed out across the cold, snow-covered landscape. I hoped the main building could contain it.

As I ran through the snow, shallow in some spots but nearly up to my knees in others, something caught my eye. Moving from around the main base toward the Shed, a thin stream of black slid slowly across the surface of the snow.

I'd forgotten. It was already outside.

"It's moving toward the Shed!" I screamed, but no one responded. Those who were still outside only ran faster. "It's coming for you! Don't you see it?"

Dr. Ling neared the Shed. In the still night, she should have been able to hear me, but the hood of her suit must have muffled the sound.

I tried to call out for the young guy ahead of me. He didn't respond either.

Just before Dr. Ling reached the door leading into the Shed, she stopped. The blackness had reached her, and it slithered around her feet, slowly wrapping itself around her and climbing her legs.

I watched in horror as the blackness slid along from Dr. Ling and into the Shed.

I had never thought of myself as a coward before that day, but to my shame, I left them all. I turned and ran to the only other building on the base. When I glanced over my shoulder, the young guy had stopped in the snow, just like Dr. Ling.

I kept running.

Tap, Tap, Tap, echoed the hanger door.

I reached the small garage. A quick glance back filled me with despair—no one had moved.

Tap, Tap, Tap.

It was a little hard to see in the darkness of the night and over such a distance, but I thought both Dr. Ling and the young guy had stomped a foot with each of the taps.

I yanked open the door to the garage and rushed inside, pulling the door closed behind me. I locked it, but I was pretty sure it wouldn't make a difference. I found my flashlight and turned it on.

Tap, Tap, Tap.

The sound came faintly through the insulated walls of the garage but still loud enough to send shivers down my spine.

TAP

I ran to the window and peered outside, clenching and unclenching my fists. Across the snow, a line of black slowly moved toward me. I had nowhere else to go. Miles and miles of frozen wasteland lay in every direction.

The line of black was only twenty feet from the garage. I turned around and, with the light from my flashlight, frantically searched for something to fight it off with. I found only disappointment.

I ran back to the window and looked out. The blackness had spread. It covered the snow around the main base and Shed, and it now reached out and around the garage.

Tap, Tap, Tap.

I was surrounded.

Tap, Tap, Tap.

The sound was faint. My breathing sped up; my chest ached. My heart felt like it was about to burst.

Tap, Tap, Tap.

Still faint, but it sounded close—really close.

I moved once again to the window by the door but jumped back as the blackness slid up the glass, covering it from the outside.

In the light of the flashlight, I rushed back through the building. I swung open the door to the storage area. Dozens of crates filled the room, but they were all sealed. I'd need a crowbar to get any of them open.

I spun around. My eye caught sight of something behind the edge of one of the crates. I pulled the crate out a little, and sure enough, a crowbar leaned against the wall.

I grabbed the steel rod, gripping it like it was the only thing between me and that blackness, hoping I could defend myself.

"Tap, Tap, Tap,"

This time, it was loud.

I ran out of the storage room and slammed the door shut behind me. I panned the flashlight around the main room. No sign of the blackness.

Yet.

Tap, Tap, Tap.

It was so close. I could have sworn it was right next to me.

Tap, Tap, Tap.

No doubt now. It was in the room with me.

Tap, Tap, Tap.

I turned around. A crate sat beside me. I shone the flashlight all around it. No sign of anything unusual.

My heart screamed in agony, and I cried out in fear as I heard it again.

Tap, Tap, Tap.

I watched as my hand, as if controlled by something else, reached out with the crowbar. On the crate, I beat out the rhythm.

Tap, Tap, Tap.

I felt at peace. A smile crept onto my face, and the crowbar dropped from my hand. Something pleasant, warm, and good swirled around my feet.

I would be okay. I was safe.

I gave myself to the darkness, and all the light went out.

Don't Forget to Check out:

THE RIDGE SERIES

  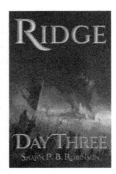

For fans of Epic Fiction, this series will grab your attention and draw you into a whole new world!

…an epic dystopian fantasy with a heavy dose of action. ...Ridge: Day One is a brilliant start to a fascinating series!" *Rabia Tanveer, Reader's Favorite*

"Ridge: Day One is a startling adult debut written with excellent style and stunning precision. Not a mark is missed, not a page lets you down." *Nathaniel Luscombe, hecticreadinglife*

"WOW, this is a fantasy thriller filled with action and surprises." *Delphia, Goodreads Reviewer*

"The plot of Ridge is clever and exciting with lots of twists and turns… Ridge: Day One is an intelligent dark fantasy that gives its readers a true hero on a quest worth cheering for." *Scott Cahan, Author of Caged Animals and the Glazed Man series*

Check out these books by

Shawn P. B. Robinson

Adult Fiction (Fantasy/Sci-Fi)

<u>Ridge Series</u>
Ridge Day One
Ridge Day Two
Ridge Day Three

ADA Anthology

Books for Younger Readers

<u>Annalynn the Canadian Spy Series</u>
Books One through Six

<u>Jerry the Squirrel Series</u>
Volumes I, II, & III
Hat Squirrel's Revenge

<u>The Arestana Quest Series</u>
The Key Quest
The Defense Quest
The Harry Quest

<u>Activity Books</u>
Jerry the Squirrel Activity Book
Annalynn the Canadian Spy Activity Book

www.shawnpbrobinson.com/books